LET'S PLAY AUTOPSY

by

Susan L. Paré

Susan L. Pare'

Copyright

This book is a work of fiction. Names, characters, places, and incidents are either a product of the author's imagination or are used fictionally. Any resemblance to actual persons, living or dead, or the actual events or locales is entirely coincidental.

Cover designed by Susan L. Pare'

Paperback ISBN– 978-0-9966195-3-0

Susan L. Pare'

<u>More Books by SUSAN L. PARE'</u>

Red

The House on Ludington Street

What's Behind the Screen Door?

The Mayor's Son

Willerton Woods

Cowtown

Floating Face Down

A Bad Week In Hollister

Don't Smother Your Mother

Crossing Sydney

Blueberries and Bears and My Brother's Shoes

Susan L. Pare'

Dedication

To my son, Jon – He reads every word, finds my errors, and respectively suggests corrections.

I also want to thank him for sharing his dog, Floyd, with me. My life is better with him in it. The dog, I mean. Well, my son, too. But, mostly the dog. Maybe they're equal. It's a coin toss. Anyway, thanks, Jon.

Contents

Let's Play Autopsy

Susan L. Pare'

One

1999

When Albert was only three years old, his father looked at a big old oak tree, growing in a field behind his house, and decided to build his son a treehouse. It took him a year to build it. It took another year before Albert was big enough to climb the rope ladder to gain access to it.

The treehouse was big and it was sturdy. For the next six years, it was a clubhouse for six kids, who had been friends since first grade. They met there after school and on weekends and shared everything with each other. When one was hurting, the rest were there to give comfort.

As they grew older, so did the games they played. By the age of eleven, they were already bored with playing chess and board games, like Trivial Pursuit. They experimented with smoking cigarettes and laughed at each other when they choked, coughed, or puked. They took turns drinking cans of beer, stolen from their parents' refrigerators, and the boys acted tough as they smashed the empties on their foreheads. Dirty magazines, also stolen from parents, educated the three boys and three girls about their growing bodies and sex. All six children were extremely intelligent and did well in school. They were devoted to each other and, as kids will do, pinky swore to be friends until death.

It was a hot summer day in Kalispell, MT. The six kids were sitting in the treehouse, drinking soda and discussing what to do over the next couple of months. They were only two weeks into their summer break and were already bored.

"We could go to the pool a few times a week," said Brad.

"My mom won't let me swim at the park. She says the pool is full of diseases and pee. 'If you want to swim, swim in your own pool. That's why we have it,' is what I hear, every time I ask her if I can go to the park," remarked Peter.

"I think we should decide about Donna and Henry," said Albert. "Do we want two more members or not?"

"We've known them for a long time," replied Emma. "I just don't know how well they'll fit in. We could do a probation thing. You know, give it a few weeks, and see how it works out."

"I've got an idea," said Sarah. "Let's put them through an initiation. If they pass the initiation, then they can join and be on probation until school starts."

"That sounds good. I like that idea. What about the rest of you? Want to vote?" asked Emma. "I say yea."

"Yea," said Peter and Albert, at the same time.

"Okay, with me," said Brad.

"Yea," said Sarah.

"I guess," said Wendy.

"You're not sure, Wendy?" said Peter. "What's wrong?"

"I'm just not sure about bringing in two more. I have a funny feeling about this," she replied.

"That's why we'll do the initiation and probation first. If it doesn't work, they're out," said Brad.

"I know," Wendy replied. "It's just - well, if it doesn't work out and we kick them out, they're going to know a lot of our secrets and stuff. I just don't know if we should do it."

"How about we do the initiation and then see what happens? We can make it tough and swear them to secrecy."

"Okay, I guess we can do that," Wendy replied. "What are we going to do for initiation?"

"I think we should play autopsy," said Emma.

"What's that?" asked Peter.

"It's kinda like playing doctor, except it's with a dead person.

Two

Wendy Berg, Peter Mont, Albert Freeman, Brad Weiss, Emma Lockhart, and Sarah Compton were sitting in sized-down versions of beanbag chairs. Henry Pullman and Donna Mason were sitting on the wooden floor, listening to Sarah as she explained the rules of the club.

"First, we never tell our parents or anybody anything we do or say here. When we are asked, we tell them we were playing some kind of a game or helping each other with schoolwork. Whatever. You must swear you will never talk about what goes on here."

"What's so bad that we can't talk about it?" asked Donna.

"You'll find out if we let you join," Sarah told her. "Two, you must agree to pay $2.00 a month for dues. We use the money for snacks and other things we need for the clubhouse. Third, . . . Now what?"

"How am I supposed to get $2.00 a week? I don't even get an allowance," asked Donna.

"That's your problem. If you want to be a member, you need to pay your dues. Steal it out of your mother's purse, if you have to. I don't care where it comes from. And, quit interrupting me," Sarah yelled at her.

"Sorry."

"Third, you never bring anyone here. No one, except us, is allowed in the clubhouse. The fourth and final rule is this. You will do everything we tell you to do until you are off probation. If you refuse, you're gone."

"How long is probation?" asked Henry.

"Until we tell you it's over," said Sarah.

"I thought we agreed it would be over when we go back to school," commented Peter.

"Well, now it's going to be when we decide it's over. No time limit," Sarah told him.

"So," asked Brad, "Do you agree to live by these rules?"

"Yes," Donna and Henry said in unison.

"Do you swear that you will never talk about our club to anyone?" Brad asked.

"Yes," replied Donna.

"Yes," said Henry.

"Good. You are now temporary members until you complete your initiation. Then, you will be on probation until we tell you that probation is over. You understand?" asked Brad.

"I do," said Donna.

"Yes," said Henry.

"What is the initiation?" asked Donna.

"You will be informed at the proper time. Until then, you may only speak when spoken to. You may not talk to anyone unless they talk to you first. This includes your parents, brothers, and sisters. Do you understand?" asked Sarah.

Donna and Henry just looked at her and said nothing.

"Do you understand?" Sarah asked them again.

"Yes?" said Donna, not sure if she should talk or not.

"Henry?"

"Yes. I understand," he finally replied.

"What's the name of the club?" asked Donna.

Albert reached over and slapped her on the side of her head. "What part of no talking don't you understand, bitch?"

Three

When Albert's father built the treehouse, he went for big and big it was. Each kid had their own small beanbag chair, which were gifts to Albert and his friends from Albert's parents. The rest of the stuff in the clubhouse were things that the kids had rescued from the neighbors' garbage. Besides the six chairs, there were two small plastic tables, an old camping cooler, and a couple of rusty, fold-up-type lawn chairs. A lot of comic books, assorted magazines, old books, and a few Playboy magazines were stored in an old wooden crate. Another old box held a blanket and an afghan, which Wendy had found in the attic of her parents' home and 'borrowed'. An old, rarely used broom stood by the doorway.

Sarah and Albert were sitting in their chairs waiting for the rest of the kids to show up. Albert was reading a comic book, while Sarah stared at him.

"What?" Albert asked. "You see something you like?"

"You wish," laughed Sarah.

"Have you decided what we're going to do?"

"I think we should scare the crap out of them," replied Sarah.

"Wendy still doesn't like the idea," said Albert.

"She doesn't like change," Sarah told him. "They're here. Throw down the ladder."

Albert got up, walked the couple of steps to the door, and threw down the rope ladder.

One at a time, Wendy, Peter, Brad, and Emma climbed up the ladder and took their seats.

"Is there anything to drink?" asked Emma.

"There's some soda in the cooler," said Albert. "It's cold, too. I brought some ice from our freezer."

"Did you raise the ladder?" asked Sarah.

"Always do," said Emma.

"Okay, guys. We have to figure out what this initiation is going to be. We can't act as if it's a big deal and then wimp out. Any ideas, anyone?" asked Albert.

"I already told you," Emma replied. "We should play Autopsy."

"What the hell is that?" Peter asked.

"Haven't any of you watched CSI? They always show a dead body, on a table, either just cut open or just sewed shut. We could make them pretend they are dead, blindfold them, and tell them we are going to cut them open. That should scare the crap out of them."

"That's stupid," said Wendy.

"What's your idea, then?" asked Emma.

"I don't know. But, not that."

"We'd get to see Donna naked," remarked Brad. "I like that idea."

"She won't be naked," said Emma.

"She'll have to be a little naked if we are going to pretend we are cutting her chest open, won't she?" asked Brad.

"We can make her take her top off. But, that's all Brad. You're such a pervert," Emma told him.

"I don't like it," said Wendy.

"Well, I do," replied Brad. "I think we should vote."

Everyone shouted yea, except Wendy.

"The yeas have it," said Brad. "Let's plan on how we are going to do this."

"We should do it when it's dark out. You know, to make it scarier. And, we'll need lots of candles," said Sarah.

"How about we show them a knife before we blindfold them and then we can use markers or a pen to pretend we are cutting them," chimed in Emma.

"The blindfolds need to be really dark, so they can't see anything," added Sarah.

"I'll get a scalpel from my father's office. That will really scare them," said Peter.

"Everyone bring some candles and I'll get the

markers," said Emma. "Wendy, you okay with this?"

"Not really. It kind of scares me. You know. Seeing a naked boy and all."

"Nobody is going to be naked. We're just going to make them take their tops off," said Peter. "You should learn to listen better, Wendy. You always get things mixed up."

"You mean you've never seen your brother naked?" asked Emma.

"Well, ya. But he was just a little kid then. This is different," Wendy replied.

"Wendy, do you want Henry to be naked?" asked Peter. "We could make him take all his clothes off."

"You can be the one who tickles it if you want. I'm sure Henry will enjoy that," Emma said, making everyone laugh.

"When are we going to do this?" asked Brad.

"I think we should do it when there's a full moon," said Emma.

"Screw that. I don't want to wait. Besides, I don't even know when that is. The sooner the better," said Brad.

"You just want to see a real half-naked girl," laughed Sarah.

"Damn right," replied Brad. "She's got tits and I

want to see them."

"One week from today," said Sarah. "We'll tell Donna and Henry they are to be here in one week. That should give us enough time to get all the stuff we need."

"It also gives them one week to worry about what's going to happen to them," said Peter.

"All agreed, say yea," said Brad.

Everyone shouted yea.

The pile of supplies grew as the week went on. The kids brought every color and type of candle they could find. Sarah brought a butane fireplace lighter to light the candles and two strips of black material to use as blindfolds. Emma brought two red and two black markers. Peter was true to his word, stole a scalpel from his father, and cut his thumb when he tested its sharpness.

Two days before the initiation, Sarah and Emma walked to a resale shop in town and bought two used throw rugs. They planned to put the rugs on opposite ends of the clubhouse, for Henry and Donna to lie down on.

Sarah, Brad, and Albert were in the clubhouse

talking about the initiation.

"Do you think they'll pass it?" Albert asked.

"Who cares? Even if they do, we still aren't going to let them join. I wish we had told Wendy that we are just planning to have some fun with them. She's so nice, though, that she might say something and ruin it," replied Sarah.

"Probably," said Brad. "And, ruin me from seeing Donna's tits."

"Is that all you think about? You really are a pervert," said Sarah.

"You want to show us your tits?" asked Albert.

"You know what? You'll see my tits when pigs fly. What's wrong with you two anyway?" Sarah asked.

"I'm sorry, Sarah," said Albert. "I didn't mean that. It's just this initiation thing. I guess we're all excited about it."

"Well, you don't hear us girls talking like that. Anyway, just stop talking about tits, will you?"

"Yes, mother," replied Brad, cracking them up.

Four

At one o'clock on Saturday afternoon, Wendy, Emma, and Sarah met at the clubhouse to get things ready for the initiation. They swept the floor and placed a throw rug at each end of the clubhouse, for Donna and Henry to lie on. They set candles on top of boxes, the two tables, and all over the floor. Once they were satisfied that everything was in place and ready for the evening, they left the clubhouse.

The six friends gathered at around seven o'clock and waited. They were excited and talked about what they were going to do and laughed at things that weren't funny. Henry and Donna were to arrive by eight o'clock sharp and wait on the ground by the tree until someone told them to climb up the ladder.

It was obvious that Wendy was a nervous wreck and Brad wouldn't stop talking about tits.

"Wendy, you have to settle down. This isn't a big deal. No one is going to get hurt," Sarah told her.

"I don't like this. I think we should just forget it. I didn't want them to join to begin with," she replied.

"It's just a joke," said Sarah. "We aren't going to let them join. This is for fun. I'm sorry we didn't tell you before, but we thought you would ruin it."

"Are you serious? All this time you knew this was a joke and didn't tell me? What kind of a friend are you, anyway?"

"We figured you would tell them. We didn't mean to hurt your feelings. It's just that you're so nice, we figured you would say something to them," replied Sarah.

"So, all of you knew this is a joke except me?" Wendy asked.

"Sorry," said Sarah.

"I'm sorry, too," Emma added.

"We're all sorry," Brad told her. "Don't be mad."

"You know what? I am mad and I'm leaving. You guys go ahead and have your mean old fun. I don't want any part of it," Wendy told them, tears running down her cheeks. "I'm out of here."

"Please don't go, Wendy," said Peter.

Wendy stood up, looked at her friends, and shook her head in disgust. Without another word, she left the clubhouse.

"Wow," said Albert. "She's really pissed. I've never seen Wendy get so upset. Maybe we should call it off."

"No. We're doing it," said Sarah. "She'll come around. Give her a few days and she'll be over it."

"It's time to get ready," said Emma. "Let's light the candles."

The clubhouse looked spooky with just the candles burning. Donna Mason was lying on one of the throw rugs, completely covered by a blanket. She could hear, but not see what was happening. Sarah had told her to lay there and not move.

Henry Pullman was lying on a throw rug on the other side of the clubhouse. He was shirtless. Peter stood over him, holding the scalpel.

"You are dead, Henry. You cannot move. We are going to perform an autopsy on you. You see this scalpel? We are going to use it to cut you open. We are going to look at your guts. If you move, you will not pass your initiation. Do you understand?"

"Yes," replied Henry.

"We are going to blindfold you now. Do not move," Peter told him.

Emma took one of the black cloth blindfolds, placed it over his eyes, and tied it behind his head.

"Can you see anything?" asked Brad.

"No."

Sarah took the red marker and knelt down beside Henry. She touched his stomach with her finger and he jumped.

"You must not move. You are dead, remember?" she said.

"Sorry," Henry told her.

She poked him hard in the stomach. "You don't talk when you're dead either, idiot."

Sarah started to draw a 'y' on his chest with the marker. As soon as she pressed down on his body, Henry jumped again.

"Are we going to have to hold you down?" asked Brad.

"Give me the knife. I'll cut him open," said Albert, winking at Peter.

"Be careful," said Peter, as he handed him the scalpel. "It's really sharp. I already cut myself with it."

Albert took the knife and started to run it across Henry's chest. The minute Henry felt the cold metal of the scalpel touch his skin, he yelled at Albert to stop. Before anyone realized what was happening, Albert made a small incision right below Henry's breastbone. Henry screamed and started to sit up. Albert pushed him back down onto the carpet and stuck the scalpel deep into Henry's belly button.

"Albert, stop," screamed Sarah. "What are you doing?"

Albert looked at her with a puzzled look on his face, then looked down at Henry, and dropped the scalpel. "I didn't mean it. I don't know what happened. I didn't mean it," he said.

Donna, frightened by the sounds she could hear, but not see, pulled her blanket off and tossed it aside. The blanket hit one of the candles, which fell over onto the box of magazines and books.

Henry was trying to get up, blood seeping out of his two wounds.

"Let me up," Henry yelled. "I want to get out of here right now."

"You can't leave. You're bleeding. Albert, do you have any gauze or bandages?" asked Emma.

"You are in so much trouble," Donna interrupted. "Just wait until I tell what you did."

"If you say one word, either one of you, you're gonna be sorry," said Albert. "I mean it. I'll. . ."

He glanced up and saw flames coming from the burning magazines and books. The blanket, lying next to the books, had started smoldering and smoke was filling the air.

"The books are on fire," Albert yelled. "What did you do, Donna? Are you crazy?"

"I'm sorry. I didn't mean to," Donna said.

"You've ruined everything," Albert screamed. He shoved her, causing her to fall back onto the smoldering blanket.

"We've got to get out of here," yelled Emma.

"No," Albert yelled back at her. "We've got to try to put the fire out. Get some water or soda."

"Everyone out," screamed Sarah.

"No. We've got to save the clubhouse," Albert yelled.

It didn't take much. The summer had been hot with little rain, and the fire, kindled by the dried-out paper, burnt fast. Barely able to see through the dense smoke, Sarah headed towards the door, opened it, and threw down the ladder. She climbed down. Henry and Brad followed her. They saw Emma come out and start to reach for the ladder, which had now started to burn.

"The ladder's on fire," Emma screamed. "How do I get down?"

"Jump, Emma. We'll catch you," yelled Brad.

Emma hesitated and looked down at her three friends. "You better catch me," she yelled, closed her eyes, and jumped. Brad and Henry caught her and the three tumbled to the ground, shook up but not hurt.

"Albert," Sarah screamed. "Albert, where are

you?"

Suddenly, Albert appeared in the doorway. "Is everyone out?" he yelled, rubbing his eyes.

"Donna and Peter are still in there," yelled Brad.

"I've got to help them," said Albert.

"No - you've got to jump. Now!"

Albert looked behind him, saw flames shooting out towards him, and jumped, breaking a leg as he hit the ground.

In minutes, flames had completely engulfed the treehouse. The screams of seven children, two of them burning to death, filled the air.

Albert's father heard screams, looked out the kitchen window, and saw the fire. He yelled at his wife to call the fire department and ran to the children.

Five

<u>2015</u>

Sarah Compton swung her big leather chair around and gazed out the window. Her office was on the 15th floor of the federal building and the view of downtown Helena was spectacular. Working as an ADA had its perks, even if the money wasn't that great. She had been hired five years ago, right out of college, and had moved up the ladder faster than she thought possible. Of course, the fact that three of the five previous ADAs were now sitting in jail had certainly helped.

She loved her boss, State's Attorney Michel Taylor, who had been appointed to the position almost fifteen years ago. Between the two of them, they handled all the high-profile cases. There were few that they did not win, and right now they were batting a healthy 97% average.

She figured Taylor would be around for another ten years or so. Then, if she played her cards right, the job would be hers. She planned on being the youngest State's Attorney in Montana history.

The intercom buzzing brought her back from her daydreaming. She turned her chair and pushed the button on the phone.

"Yes, Amy," she said.

"Sarah, there's a Mister Lockhart on the phone. Do you want to speak to him?"

"That doesn't ring a bell. Can you find out what it's about?"

A couple of seconds later, Amy was back on the line. "He said he's the father of Emma. He said you went to school with her."

Sarah hesitated, not sure if she wanted to take his call. "Take a message. I'll call him back," Sarah finally said.

Sarah looked at the pile of folders on her desk. She had tons of work to do. I don't have time for this right now, she thought. But, instead of opening the folder in front of her, she turned her chair and gazed out of the window again.

She thought of Emma who had barely made it through high school. The last time Sarah had seen her was at their high school graduation. Sarah had heard stories about Emma being depressed and trying to kill herself, but she had no idea if they were true. Now, Emma's father was calling her and she didn't want to talk to him. She was afraid of what he had to say.

The intercom buzzed again. Sarah ignored it. It buzzed again and she pushed the button. "What is it now?" she practically yelled at Amy.

"Sorry, boss. It's that Mr. Lockhart again. He said that he really needs to speak with you. He left a message and asked that you call him as soon as possible."

"What does the message say?" Sarah asked.

"It says, 'Emma is dead. The police think she killed herself, but I'm sure she was murdered. I found her diary. Call me back. I think I should talk to you before I turn it over to the police.'"

"Was that it?" Sarah asked her.

"Who's Emma?" Amy asked.

"Not important. Give me the number."

"Are you going to call him back? This almost sounds like a threat to me," Amy said.

"No, it doesn't. It's just the way he talks. He's the father of a girl I went to school with. She's had a lot of problems. I doubt she was murdered, though."

"So, are you going to call him?" Amy asked again.

"Probably. Just not right now. If he calls again, tell him I'm out of the office for the rest of the day," said Sarah. She hit the intercom button and cut off their conversation.

What the hell did Emma write in that diary,

Sarah wondered. It had to be important if her father was planning on turning it over to the police, she thought. Sarah actually felt sick to her stomach for a moment, thinking she was going to throw up. She took a couple of deep breaths and settled herself down. After a few minutes, she picked up her cell phone and made a call.

"Sarah Jane. Haven't heard from you for a while. What's up, girl?"

"Hey, Brad. How are you doing?"

"I'm fine. Business is booming. I'm telling you, Sarah, tits have made me rich."

"Your dead grandmother made you rich," Sarah said.

Brad laughed. "I have to admit, it sure helped to get me started in this business. But I'm telling you it's the boobs that keep me living the fine life. Did you know that I have never seen two sets of tits that look the same? They are all different and they are all beautiful."

"My god, Brad, will you ever grow up?" Sarah asked, still laughing. "I don't think you've changed one bit since you were twelve."

"I sure hope I never grow up," Brad replied. "So, what can I do for you this fine day?"

"I just got a call from Emma's dad."

"Emma? You mean Emma Lockhart?" Brad asked.

"Yes. I didn't talk to him, but he left a message for me to call him. Emma's dead. She killed herself."

"My god, that's terrible," Brad exclaimed.

"Her father thinks she was murdered."

"What? That's ridiculous. Who would want to kill her? Anyway, we know she tried it a couple of times before and failed. Sounds like she succeeded this time."

"Her father found her diary. He said he wanted to talk to me before he turned it over to the police," Sarah told him.

The phone went quiet. "Brad, are you there?"

"I'm here. You don't think it has anything about the fire in it, do you?" he asked.

"I don't know. I know I have to call him back and I'm afraid of what he's going to tell me."

"Okay. Calm down. It could be anything. Let's not get ahead of ourselves. You are an attorney. Maybe he just needs some advice about something. Give him a call and see what he's got to say."

"I don't want to call him while I'm at work. Too many interruptions. I'll call him tonight."

"Let me know what you find out," said Brad. "And, quit worrying. It's probably nothing."

"You're right. I'm probably worrying for no reason. I'll call you later this evening. Bye, now."

"Bye."

Sarah sat for a few minutes, thinking about what Emma's father could want. She couldn't remember the last time something had shaken her up this bad. She pushed the intercom button.

"What do you need, boss?" Amy asked.

"Call Mr. Lockhart back. Tell him I'm tied up for the rest of the day but I'll give him a call this evening."

"Will do. What if he wants to know what time? What should I tell him?"

"Tell him I'll call him around eight. Thanks, Amy."

Six

"Hello."

"Mr. Lockhart, this is Sarah Compton calling. I'm so sorry to hear about Emma. My prayers are with you and your family."

"Thank you, Sarah. And, thanks for getting back to me."

"Your message was kind of confusing. What happened?"

"Emma was found around 5:30 yesterday morning in Forest Valley Park. Some joggers found her sitting on a park bench. At first, they thought she was sleeping, but then they noticed all the blood."

"That's terrible."

"It's devastating. Her mother and I are heartbroken. You know Emma had emotional problems. She was never the same after that horrible fire. She rarely left the house after she graduated from high school."

"Yes, I know it was hard on her. I heard some stories over the years that she was depressed."

"That's putting it mildly. She tried suicide twice, which is why the police are now saying she killed herself. But I know she didn't. I know she was murdered."

"What makes you think that? I'm sure the police must have some good reasons to have come to that conclusion," Sarah said.

"Emma never left the house unless it was absolutely necessary. I think she was meeting someone."

"Did you hear her leave?"

"That's the thing. Her mom and I went to bed early – around 9:30 - and I know she was in her room at that time. When I got up, around 3:00 to go to the bathroom, she wasn't in her room. I just figured she was down in the family room watching TV. She did that a lot. She had trouble sleeping."

"So, you didn't hear her leave the house?" Sarah inquired.

"No. She could have left any time after her mother and I went to bed."

"What makes you think she was meeting someone?"

"I checked her phone. She had a call at 10:15. It only lasted a few minutes."

"Did you mention this to the police?"

"Of course, but they weren't concerned. They had already come to the conclusion that she had killed herself."

"Due to her past history," Sarah stated.

"Exactly," Mr. Lockhart said. "I might have agreed except for a couple of things."

"What were they?" Sarah asked.

"I found her diary."

"Emma still kept a diary?"

"No. This was from when you were kids. When you all still hung around with each other."

Sarah's heart was beating fast. Dear god, she thought, what did Emma write in that book? Please, please, don't let it be about the fire. "That's so long ago," she said. "I barely remember those days."

"I found a piece of paper sticking out of the diary. It was dated yesterday. All it said was, 'If anything happens to me, call Sarah.'"

"It says you should call me?" Sarah asked.

"Yes. Do you know why she would do that? Why did she want me to call you?"

"Mr. Lockhart, I have no idea. Have you read the diary?"

"Not all of it. It's mostly the ramblings of a sweet little girl. It's too hard – it's just so very hard," he said, his voice cracking.

"I'm so sorry, Mr. Lockhart."

"She met someone at the park. I'm sure of it.

She had to be afraid, right? Otherwise, why would she write that note? Can you think of any reason someone would hurt my little girl?"

"I wish I could help you. Emma and I drifted apart years ago. It's been ten years since I've seen her. I don't know what she meant by the note and I certainly don't know why someone would want to hurt her. Perhaps the police are right and she did take her own life."

"No! It doesn't add up. Yes, she tried to kill herself before, but she took pills. She couldn't stand the sight of blood. Yet, both her wrists were slit. She would never have done that."

"She slit her wrists?" Sarah asked.

"She was found with her wrists slit, but I'll never believe that she did it," Mr. Lockhart replied.

"What do you want me to do? How can I help you?"

"Would you check around and see if anyone knows anything? Maybe if you talk to her friends – you know, the kids you hung around with – well, maybe someone knows something.

"I can do that. Do you remember Brad Weiss? He lives here in Helena. We're still in touch and I'm certain he hasn't heard from Emma in years. I can check with the others, though, and see what I can find out."

"I'd appreciate it if you would do that, Sarah. Needless to say, her mother and I are overwhelmed. Something is just not right about this whole thing."

"When is the funeral, Mr. Lockhart? Have you made any arrangements yet?"

"It's private. We do not want any flowers if that's what you're thinking."

"I was thinking of trying to get off work and drive up for the funeral."

"Don't bother. It's closed to everyone except immediate family."

"Mr. Lockhart, I have an idea. It's just a thought and it's up to you. I'd like to read her diary. I wonder if she put that note in it so that I would check it out. Perhaps, there's something in there that would make sense to me and not to you."

"That's an idea. Let me take down your address and I'll mail it to you. I want it back though."

"Of course. In the meanwhile, I'll get in touch with the others and see if they know anything."

"There's one other thing I should mention," Mr. Lockhart said.

"What's that?"

"The police told me that her wrists weren't cut with a knife."

"Well, it's common for people to use a razor blade. They're a lot sharper."

"No, listen to me. The police found a scalpel next to her body. Her wrists were cut with a scalpel. It doesn't make any sense. And, tell me, where in the world would Emma have gotten a scalpel?"

Seven

As soon as Sarah finished her call with Emma's dad, she called Brad.

"What did her old man have to say?" Brad asked.

"She was found dead on a park bench at 5:30 in the morning."

"Who found her?" Brad inquired.

"That's not important – some joggers, I guess. Anyway, the police are calling it suicide. She left a note in an old diary asking her father to get in touch with me if anything happened to her."

"Why you?"

"I have no idea. He's mailing me the diary to see if I can figure it out. Anyway, this is the scary part, Brad. She slit her wrists. She bled out."

"No way! Emma couldn't stand the sight of blood. Do you remember when Wendy fell and cut her leg? Emma almost passed out when she saw blood. Another time she . . . "

"I know," Sarah interrupted. "But here's the thing that's disturbing. They found a scalpel next to her body. The police said she cut her wrists with a scalpel."

"Well, I guess it's possible that she used one. I

find it kind of hard to believe, though," Brad said.

"Exactly. Her father said there was no way she would have cut her wrists. He said she took pills the other times she tried to kill herself and she didn't have access to any medical supplies."

"I guess she could have ordered one or maybe she went to the doctor and took one from his office."

"Seriously, Brad? How many times have you seen scalpels just lying around in a doctor's office? Never. That's how many. I think that scalpel was a warning."

"A warning for what?" Brad asked.

"I don't know. But, why would Emma ask her dad to call me if something happened to her? Maybe she was being threatened. And, she did get a phone call at 10:15 that night. She was probably meeting someone."

"Who would she be meeting? I know – you don't know. I don't know what I'm supposed to do with this information, Sarah. We haven't talked to Emma in years. How are we supposed to know what was going on in her life? This is crazy. I say just stay out of it."

"I can't. I promised her father I would check with the old gang and see if they knew anything," Sarah replied.

"Well, I, for one, don't want any part of it."

"Tough cookies, my friend. Because you are going to help me with this."

"I am?"

"Yes, you are. I want you to get in touch with Albert and Henry. Find out if they know anything. I'll call Wendy and see if she has heard anything."

"Come on, Sarah. This isn't any of our business. Anyway, why would Henry know anything? It's not like he was part of our gang. I don't have time for this crap."

"Then, take time. You call them and make sure you ask the right questions. Let's see what's going on."

"I don't understand why you're so obsessed with this. Emma was off her rocker and she killed herself. End of story. Her old man is just grasping at straws, trying to convince everyone that she didn't commit suicide."

"What if she didn't, Brad? What if this has something to do with the fire? What if her father is right and she was murdered?"

"I doubt that very much, but if it will make you feel better I'll call Albert. But I don't want to talk to Henry."

"Fine. I'll call him and Wendy and see if they

know anything. I've got a bad feeling about this," Sarah said.

"Hey, kiddo. You're the tough one, remember? Just relax, will you? This has nothing to do with us. That fire was sixteen years ago."

"I know. It's just that – well, I just have this feeling – I don't know – it's just that ever since Mr. Lockhart called, I've had this horrible premonition that something really bad is going to happen."

"She wasn't murdered and her death has nothing to do with that damn old fire."

"I hope you're right. But, what if it does? What if someone found out what really happened? Remember, that damn game was Emma's idea in the first place."

"I've had enough of your jibber-jabber for one night. I'll talk to you later. Love ya, Sarah. And, just relax, will you?"

Sarah stared at her phone. Brad had hung up on her. Maybe I am being paranoid, she thought. But Emma's father sounded so sure that his daughter hadn't killed herself. The fact that she was found dead in a park, early in the morning with a scalpel next to her, was enough to convince Sarah that this was no suicide.

She turned on the TV and tried to concentrate on the news. Her mind kept picturing Emma and how sad she looked the last time she had seen her. Losing two friends in that fire had changed them all, in one way or the other. Emma never forgave herself for suggesting that stupid made-up game and blamed herself for what had happened. She probably did kill herself, Sarah thought. It's just that there's too much evidence that points in a different direction.

She turned off the TV and stared out her living room window into the darkness.

Eight

The next morning Sarah received Emma's diary, which Mr. Lockhart had overnighted to her. It surprised her that he had sent it so quickly. He must really think there's something important in it, she thought.

Stuck between the pages, in the middle of the book, was a note which read, "Sarah, this is as far as I read. Perhaps you can find something that can explain what happened. I know Emma didn't kill herself. Arthur Lockhart."

Sarah flipped through the diary. At least I'll get a chance to see if Emma wrote anything about the fire, she thought. If she did, this book is definitely going to have one serious accident. She put the diary in her purse, deciding she would read it that night after she arrived home from work, and before she called Wendy and Henry.

"Everyone knows she killed herself, Sarah," Wendy said. "She tried it a couple of times before. It was like she took just enough pills to get attention, but never enough to kill herself. It was just a matter of time before she got serious about it."

"Her father sent me her diary," Sarah told

Wendy.

"Why would he do that?"

"He thinks there might be a clue in it as to who murdered her. I wanted him to send it to me so I could read it and find out if she wrote anything about the fire."

"Was there?"

"Yes, but it doesn't say anything about how it started or any of that other stuff. She just wrote that the treehouse burned down and that she lost some friends. That was the last entry. She never wrote in it again."

"So, are you coming back for the funeral?" Wendy asked her.

"No. Mr. Lockhart said it's private and for family only."

"I didn't know that," said Wendy. "I've been waiting to hear something. Well, it's probably just as well. You know, with how she died and all."

"Wendy, did you ever talk to her?"

"It's been years since we had a real conversation. I ran into her a couple of times and said hi, but it was just in passing."

"So, you don't know of anyone who would want to hurt her?"

"Want to hurt her? Of course not. You're not buying into her father's story about her being murdered, are you?"

"It just seems weird, you know. Why was she out in the middle of the night and found on a park bench with her wrists slit open? Where did she get the scalpel she used? Too many unanswered questions, if you ask me. Something's not right with that whole picture."

"Wait a minute," said Wendy. "That wasn't in the paper. It didn't mention the way she died. Are you sure that's what happened? We all thought she took pills. She used a scalpel?"

"Yes. One was found next to her body. The police told Mr. Lockhart that she used it to cut her wrists."

"Sarah, you're scaring me. There is no way Emma would do that. We all figured she took pills again. Oh, my god. Did she use a scalpel?"

"Yes. Remember, it was her idea to play the autopsy game that night. Peter brought the scalpel."

"What are you saying, Sarah?"

"I'm not sure. I'm probably just paranoid, but I have this horrible feeling that Emma isn't going to be the last one to die under suspicious circumstances."

Sarah's conversation with Henry Pullman was

basically a repeat of her conversation with Wendy. He was just as surprised as Wendy had been when Sarah told him about the scalpel. "I'll be damned," he exclaimed. "That puts a different light on things, you know. I've never told anyone about what led up to the fire that night, so I know it didn't come from me. About the scalpel, that is. I doubt anyone has talked about it, Sarah. We all swore we would never tell anyone. I wish I could tell you something that would help but I'm sure Mr. Lockhart is just upset about Emma's death. I think it would be easier for him to accept her being gone if someone killed her. It's a lot easier than trying to face the fact that she killed herself. I don't think there's anything to find that is going to say different."

"I guess you're right. I'll give him a call tomorrow. Brad is going to call Albert to see if he knows anything, but I'm sure that's a dead end."

"How is Tits doing anyway?"

"Tits? Since when do you call him Tits?" Sarah said laughing.

"We started calling him that in grade school. All the guys called him that. He sure loved to look at those boobies."

"Still does. I can't believe I never knew his nickname. He sure went into the right business. He's surrounded by boobs night and day."

"Ya. Well, being a car salesman, I'm surrounded by boobs every day, too. Just not the same kind he is. He gets to have all the fun. Most of the boobs I deal with are dumb asses."

"How is business, anyway? Still making the big bucks?"

"I can't complain. Seriously, it's pretty good. It puts food on the table. We're even talking about starting a family. We can afford it and we figure this is as good a time as any."

"That's great. You'll be a great dad, Henry."

"Tell Brad hi for me when you talk to him. Maybe I'll take a drive to Helena one of these days for a visit. We could have lunch and I could take a look at his place."

"Well, there's a lot to look at. I'd love for you to do that. Lunch is on me. There's a great little place called The Bacon Bar we could go to. You'd love it. Bacon, bacon, bacon. Everything comes with bacon. Even their sundaes."

"Sounds great. It was great talking to you, but I've got to go. Jean and I are off to the movies. Keep in touch, will you?"

"I will. Just one more question. Did you ever

hear anything about that scalpel being found after the fire?"

"Not that I recall. I never heard any conversation about it. I still have the scars, you know."

"Scars? Oh, Henry, I almost forgot about that. I'm so sorry that happened. That wasn't supposed to happen, you know."

"Calm down," Henry said, laughing. "That was sixteen years ago. We were just kids and kids do dumb things. I'm sorry I mentioned it."

"Okay, then. I'll let you go. Enjoy the movies. Bye, Henry."

"Bye, Sarah."

"Albert doesn't know anything," Brad told Sarah. "He didn't even know that Emma was dead."

"So that's it then. No one has any idea why Emma would have killed herself. What else did he have to say?"

"Well, let's see. He's still working for the town of Kalispell. He's doing more outdoor stuff now. Like changing street lights, putting up decorations for the holidays, that kind of stuff. It sounds to me like he sits on his ass in a truck most of the time, doing nothing. Those city jobs are pretty cushy. I've always wondered why it takes six guys to do something. One guy usually does the work while the other five stand around and shoot the breeze."

"Is he married?" Sarah inquired.

"Nope. But he's got a kid with some woman he used to go with. Didn't work out, but he pays her child support. He bitched about that for about five minutes. That and the fact that his leg bothers him a lot"

"The one he broke when he jumped?"

"That's the one. That's about it, I guess. Oh, ya. He hunts a lot and said he has a room full of trophies."

"Did he say anything about the rest of the guys? Does he ever see them?"

"It didn't sound like it. Wait. I almost forgot something. You're going to love this."

"What?"

"You talked to Wendy, right?"

"I told you I did."

"Did she mention anything about her love life?"

"We didn't get into it. Why? What did Albert tell you?"

"She's been seen a lot with an older man. It's, like, the talk of the town."

"For god's sake, Brad, spit it out, will you?

"It seems that our shy, sweet, innocent, wouldn't

say shit if she had a mouthful, friend Wendy has been seeing Dr. Mont."

"Get out! See's dating Peter's father? No way. Where's his wife?"

"She died a few years ago. Anyway, it seems that Wendy stayed in touch with the family after graduation. Then, after Mrs. Mont died, she really stayed in touch, if you know what I mean."

"I'll be damned. She's the last person I would ever figure doing something like that. I guess it just goes to show you that you don't know anyone and what they are capable of," Sarah said.

"You got that right. Sorry, I've got to go. I'm needed up at the bar. I'll talk to you later," Brad told her.

"Love Ya. Take care."

Nine

Detective Morris Myers watched the doorway of the church as the family of Emma Lockhart exited the building. That might have been one of the shortest funeral services ever, he thought to himself. It seemed like it had barely started before it was over.

He recognized everyone that departed the building as relatives of the Lockharts. He was hoping that some unrelated, strange person would show up but he hadn't seen anyone that didn't belong there. In some cases, it gives a killer a certain amount of satisfaction to witness his victim's funeral. Obviously, this was not one of those times.

Perhaps, he was wrong and Emma Lockhart had killed herself. The coroner certainly thought so and had decided that her death was by her own hands. But he had been on the job long enough to know a murder when he saw one. He was about as positive as a person could be that the coroner had gotten this one wrong.

He glanced in the rearview mirror of his squad car and his cold blue eyes stared back at him. He never really thought much about his looks. Women seemed to go for him and often commented on how they loved to run their fingers through his dark brown curly hair. He wondered why. It's just hair. He would never figure out what made women tick.

He started his car, intending to leave when he noticed someone driving slowly past the church. He noted the make and model of the car, wrote down the plate number, and made a mental note to check it when he got back to the station. The driver of the vehicle looked his way, saw his police car, speeded up, and drove off.

Detective Myers had immediately recognized Emma Lockhart when he had arrived at Forest Valley Park a week ago. He knew the family, though not well, and that Emma had a history of attempting suicide. He mostly remembered her, though, as a little twelve-year-old girl, sitting on the ground sobbing, as a fireman covered her with a blanket, picked her up, and carried her to an ambulance. It was a night he wished he could put behind him, but the memories of those two children being burned to death still haunted him.

He still wondered what had actually happened the night that treehouse caught on fire. What were seven kids doing in there with all those candles burning? It was a deathtrap, for certain. They all told the same story, almost word for word, and no one ever doubted them. The town was so torn up about the deaths of two children that they accepted the story of the surviving five as being true.

In his mind, even now - sixteen years later - he could see the pain that had been on the face of that little girl. It was the same look that he had seen on her face a few days ago in the park. One thing he knew for sure was that she hadn't cut her own wrists. This was no suicide. Emma Lockhart had been murdered and it was up to him to find out why.

Arthur Lockhart looked up as his wife, Caroline, entered Emma's bedroom.

"You need to come be with family, Arthur. Sitting in here all alone isn't going to do any good. She's gone and we need you with us downstairs."

"I just talked to Sarah Compton," he told her.

"What in the world for?"

"I called her a couple of days ago and asked her to see if she could find out anything about Emma and who would want to hurt her. She didn't know anything. No one she talked to knew anything."

"Oh, Arthur. No one hurt our little Emma. She took her own life. You know that. I know that. Please quit tormenting yourself. It's over. She's gone."

"She didn't kill herself!" Arthur yelled. "I don't want to live if she killed herself."

"Shhh. Please, don't yell."

"What am I going to do without her? Tell me."

"Come with me, dear." Caroline took her husband's hand. "It's best if you go to our room and lie down."

Arthur looked up at his wife and stood. "I am tired," he said, as she led him out of their dead daughter's room.

Ten

For the next two weeks, Sarah put all her energy into preparing for a trial. She couldn't figure out why the defense attorney hadn't gotten his client to agree to a plea bargain. This was a cut-and-dried case and the defendant, an absolutely adorable twenty-year-old named Sammy Jackson, had been caught on the premises by an off-duty policeman. The adorable, but terribly stupid young man had attempted to rob a gas station using the old finger-in-the-pocket trick. They had him on attempted robbery, but without a weapon, he was sure to get off with only a few years in jail. For some reason, Jackson's attorney thought he could get the kid off and had talked him into refusing a plea.

Sarah smiled. I'd let him go if I was on the jury, she thought. He's a heartbreaker, for sure. If Jackson's lawyer gets a majority-female jury, all the kid has to do is smile and they'll probably find him not guilty.

She decided to run it by her boss and see if they could make a better offer. The DA didn't like to lose and there was a good possibility that Jackson would walk on this one.

Her intercom buzzing made her jump. She laughed as she pushed the button and asked Amy what she needed.

"What are you laughing at?" Amy asked her.

"Nothing."

"You have a phone call on line six. A Mr. Brad Weiss. Do you want to take the call?" Amy asked her.

"I'll take it. Thanks."

Sarah pushed the button and connected with Brad. "What's up, Brad?"

"Sarah, have you watched the news this morning?"

"No, I've been busy working on a case. You sound weird. What's going on?"

"Turn on Channel 5."

Sarah picked up the TV remote and pushed the on button. She turned to Channel 5 and saw the Kalispell Chief of Police, John McKnight, being interviewed by a bunch of reporters.

"What am I watching?" Sarah asked Brad.

"Quiet. Just listen," he told her. "He's giving a statement."

At 1:30 a.m. Albert Freeman's body was found in his backyard. A neighbor, a retired fireman, who lives next store to Mr. Freeman, was awakened by his dog barking. He got out of bed to go to the bathroom and, as he walked by his bedroom window, he noticed a

strange glowing light coming from Albert's back yard.
He opened a bedroom window, in order to stick his
head out and get a better look, and the smell of burning
flesh filled the air. He then noticed that something was
burning in Albert's fire pit.

The neighbor pulled his blanket off his bed and
ran outside to Albert's backyard. He threw the blanket
over Albert's burning body and extinguished the fire. He
then dialed 911 and explained what had happened,
adding that there was no need to rush. He told the
emergency operator that he had seen enough bodies,
when he was on the job, to know when a person was
beyond help. That's basically all we have for now. I'll
answer one or two questions, but I've told you most of
what we already know.

Sarah said nothing while she listened to Chief
McKnight answer the reporter's questions. She felt like
someone had punched her in her stomach and she
was finding it hard to breathe.

She was about to turn off the TV, when one of
the reporters asked, "Is it true that you found a knife
sticking out of his stomach?"

Sarah stared at the screen. Please, dear god, say
no, she thought to herself. Say it isn't true.

"We aren't at liberty to say anything else at this time," the Police Chief answered.

Sarah turned off the TV. "Brad, are you still there?" she asked.

"What the fuck is going on, Sarah? That's two murders in just a few weeks."

"So, now you think that Emma was murdered?"

"Hell, yes."

"Who?"

"What?" Brad replied.

"Who would want to kill them? This doesn't make sense. Why now, after all this time?"

"I just know we better watch our backs. There are still four of us left."

"Stop it. You're scaring me, Brad."

"You better be scared. There's more. I talked to my sister this morning."

"Lori?"

"Yes. She still works at Kalispell Memorial and she was on duty when they brought Albert in. Sarah, it wasn't a knife that they found sticking out of his belly. It was a scalpel."

Eleven

Detective Myers opened the folder laying on his desk. After searching for almost thirty minutes, he had finally found the archived file, stored with hundreds of others, in the basement of the police station. The file was dated July 13, 1999. Emma Lockhart had been found dead in Forest Valley Park on July 13, 2015.

Myers spent the next few minutes reading the report. It was only a couple of pages long and the information was scarce. It simply stated that five twelve-year-old kids had asked a couple of friends to join them in their clubhouse for the evening. A few candles had been lit, as the clubhouse was dark, and some books caught fire. Two of the children, Donna Mason and Peter Mont, had not survived the fire. All of the surviving children had been transported to a local hospital.

Albert Freeman had suffered a broken leg when jumping out of the treehouse. Henry Pullman had some cuts on his chest and stomach, but could not recall how he was injured. The children were treated and released into their parents' care.

The other three children were checked out and, except for the emotional aspect of what had happened, were found in good physical condition and released.

The five had been questioned individually and all of them told the same story about what had happened. The fire was determined to be an accident and no further investigation was deemed necessary.

Myers took a sip of his cold coffee, sat back, and thought about what he had just read. Sixteen years ago, two young kids had lost their lives in a fire. Now two more of those kids were dead within weeks of each other. He was surer than ever that Emma Lockhart did not kill herself.

He picked up the phone and called Mike Johnson, a retired fireman who used to work for the Kalispell Fire Department.

Twenty minutes later, Myers poured himself a hot cup of coffee and read over his notes one more time. Mike Johnson remembered that fire like it was yesterday. He remembered the name of each child. He recalled what some of them were wearing and he remembered that Henry Pullman wasn't wearing a shirt. The fireman just assumed he had pulled it off because it had caught on fire. Although Henry didn't have any burns on his body, he had some cuts on his stomach.

After they put the fire out, the firemen sorted

through the ashes and items that had not burned and found the remnants of some bean bag chairs, a cooler, some old tray tables, and metal folding chairs. Johnson told him that there were quite a few candle holders, both metal and glass, that were scattered among the rubbish.

Johnson told Myers that was basically it. All the kids were transported to the hospital. All their statements were in the file that Myers had just read. He had nothing else to offer.

Then Myers had asked Johnson, "Did any of the firemen find any type of a weapon in the debris?"

Johnson laughed and asked him, "Do you mean a gun? What the hell are you talking about?"

Myers replied, "Did you find some kind of a knife?"

Johnson went quiet for a few seconds. "We didn't find a knife that night," he told Myers. "We went back and checked the area the next day and we did find something. We didn't think too much about it, as it was quite a distance from the treehouse. We never made a connection between it and the kids, though. No reason to."

"What the hell did you find, Mike?"

"Well, I guess it's called a scalpel. You know, like

what a doctor would use."

Detective Myers now had no doubt he was working a double homicide. Further, he did not doubt that these murders had something to do with a fire that killed two young kids sixteen years ago. It was becoming obvious that someone was avenging their deaths. But, why now?

Myers looked over the file one more time. It was Albert's treehouse. Six kids belonged to the treehouse gang, but only five of them were there when the fire started. Donna Mason and Henry Pullman were the friends who joined them.

Emma Lockhart and Albert Freeman had been murdered. That left four still living out of eight. Henry Pullman was the only one living who was not part of the original treehouse gang. That left Sarah Compton, Brad Weiss, and Wendy Berg. But Wendy Berg wasn't there when the fire started. So, why wasn't she there? Okay, Myers thought, it's time to find out where these four were on the nights of July 13th and 27th.

His first phone call was to Brad Weiss. Brad told him that he was in Helena both nights the murders took place. On July 13th he worked the bar the entire night, closed out the registers, made a late-night deposit on his way home, and enjoyed the next few hours having sex with one of his dancers. When Detective Myers asked for the name of the woman he was with, Brad hesitated.

"We need the name, Brad," Myers said. "We're going to check out your story."

"Oh, I have no problem giving you the name. I'm just not sure if it was Candi, Star, or Muffin. I kind of rotate between the three of them."

"So, you don't remember who you were with that night?"

"Not really. My routine is pretty much the same every night. I would have done the same thing on the 27th that I did on the night of the 13th. We're closed on Sundays and Mondays, but the rest of the week my routine seldom varies."

"July 13th and 27th were Mondays, Brad."

"No shit. Well, I sure as hell wasn't in Kalispell. I haven't been back there since Christmas."

"I believe you, but we still need to rule you out. Right now, everyone's a suspect."

"What do you suggest? I don't know what else to tell you. On Sundays and Mondays I golf, do some shopping, sleep late, and work out at the gym.

Basically, whatever the hell I feel like doing. I sure didn't feel like killing any of my friends, if that's what you're getting at."

"You have GPS on your car?"

"Of course. Why?"

"I'm going to ask Detective West to take a look at it. It will show if you were in town on those days. Will you agree to that?"

"Of course. Send him over," answered Brad.

Myers was told that Sarah Compton was in court when he called her. He left a message with her secretary, Amy, asking her to return his call when she was free. When Amy asked what it was about, he told her it was a private matter and hung up.

Twelve

Mrs. Lockhart asked if Detective Myers would care for a cup of coffee, stating that she had just made a fresh pot.

"That would be great. I always enjoy a fresh cup of coffee. It seems the stuff they brew at the station manages to turn to tar in no time at all."

"Have you got news about Emma?" Arthur Lockhart asked.

"Actually, I have a couple of questions. A few things are bothering me, Arthur, and I've decided to take a closer look at Emma's death. Some things don't add up and, now with Albert Freeman being murdered, I'm beginning to think you may be right. I don't think she committed suicide."

Lockhart jumped out of his chair and started pacing back and forth. "I knew it!" he exclaimed. "I knew I was right. Someone killed her, didn't they?"

"It looks like it. At least to me, it does. And, I think it has something to do with that fire sixteen years ago."

"What are you talking about?" Caroline asked as she handed Myers a cup of coffee. "How could her death have anything to do with that?"

"I'm not sure," Detective Myers said. "But I

intend to find out. I want you to tell me everything you remember about that night. Did she ever tell you why Wendy Berg wasn't there? Or, how Henry Pullman got those cuts in his stomach? Do you remember her saying anything that seemed out of the ordinary about that night?"

"Emma was never the same after that. She barely made it through high school. She would have quit but we wouldn't allow it. By the time she graduated, she wanted nothing to do with the outside world. She kept pretty much to herself from that point on," Caroline said.

"We never really gave much thought to the fact that Wendy wasn't there. It didn't come up at the time," said Arthur.

"What about the cuts on Henry's stomach?" Myers asked.

"From what I remember, he said he got cut climbing down the ladder. Later on, he changed it and said he didn't remember how it happened. There was so much confusion that night. We were just happy that Emma was okay, and didn't pay much attention to anything else," Arthur replied.

"I know she tried to kill herself a couple of times," Myers said. "Did she ever talk about why or give you a reason? Anything you remember would help?"

"It was so long ago," said Arthur. "She cried a lot. We could never bring her out of her depression. When we tried to talk to her about it, she would just shut down, saying it was all her fault and she had no right to live."

"I remember one time, right after the fire, she said that she should have been the one to die, not her friends."

"She never told you why she blamed herself?" Myers asked.

"Not really. Just what we told you," said Arthur.

"She said it wouldn't have happened if they hadn't played that dumb game," said Caroline.

"What game was that?" asked Myers.

Arthur and Caroline Lockhart looked at him, the pain of losing their child still showing on their faces. Tears ran down Caroline's cheeks. Arthur shook his head. "We have no idea," he said. "We never pushed it. She didn't want to talk about that night and we never pushed her into talking about it. We thought if we just ignored it, she would eventually let it go."

"Thank you. You've been a big help," Myers said.

Myers stood, thanked Caroline for the coffee,

shook Arthur's hand, and left.

Detective Myers drove over to John and Patricia Freeman's house. They moved shortly after the fire and had been living in a nice home on 3rd Avenue East for the past fifteen years. Patricia was home and opened the door just as he was about to ring the bell.

"Saw you drive up, Morris."

"Hi, Pat, I'm so sorry about Albert. If there is anything I can do, please don't hesitate to ask me."

"You can find the sick son of a bitch that killed my son," she yelled.

"Is John home?"

"No. He's over at the funeral parlor. I expect he'll be back in an hour or so."

"I'm not going to stay. I just have a couple of questions, if you think you're up to it."

Patricia Freeman looked up at him and gave him a sad smile. "I'm sorry I snapped. I'm not myself."

"Of course, you're not. How's John doing?"

Patricia gave a snarky laugh. "How do you think? He's devastated. You know how close he was with Albert. You need to ask questions? Here are your answers. No, no, and no. No, I don't know who would want to hurt Albert. No, I don't know where or who he was with that night. And, no, it doesn't have anything to do with Kitty. They were friends. She let him see his little girl regularly and they weren't having any problems. Does that answer your questions, Morris?"

Detective Myers didn't say anything for a second. He reached out and pulled Pat in close and hugged her. "I'm so sorry, Pat. So very, very sorry. I'm going to do my best to find the son of a bitch that killed Albert. I promise."

"I know you will, Morris."

"I know you've got a lot going on right now, but I need your help. I think these murders have something to do with the fire."

"Murders? What do you mean, murders?"

"It's looking more and more like Emma Lockhart was murdered, too."

"Oh, god, no. Morris, what's happening?"

"That's what I've got to find out. I need to know everything you remember about that night sixteen years ago. Mostly, I need to know anything that you might remember Albert said after the fire. The slightest little thing might help."

"You seriously think this has something to do with that night?"

"I do, Pat. For some reason, people are being

murdered and the only common denominator is that fire."

"Let me talk to John about this and I'll get back to you."

"Thank you. Looks like you've got more company coming up your sidewalk. I'll get going now. I'll talk to you later."

"Thanks, Morris."

"Bye, Pat."

Myers sat in his squad car and stared at the Freeman's house. For the next few days these parents, who had just lost a child, were expected to be gracious and welcoming to friends and neighbors who wanted to help. If it was me, he thought, I'd want to be alone to scream and swear and throw things. I don't think I could be as reserved as what I just experienced with Pat Freeman and the Lockharts. How do they do it, he wondered?

There is nothing I can do to bring their children back, he thought. But, I sure as hell can find their killer and see that he gets what's coming to him. What could these kids have done, sixteen years ago, that was so horrible they are now dying for it?

He started the car and drove off.

Thirteen

Albert Freeman had not been murdered in his home. There was no forensic evidence to prove otherwise.

There had, however, been marks found in his yard indicating that he had been dragged from the front of his house to the fire pit in the back yard. Blood, which had been found on numerous clumps of grass, had been analyzed and shown to be Albert's. It was determined that this had come from multiple head wounds found on the back of Albert's skull.

A hammer, found by the side of Albert's car, had no usable fingerprints on it. Forensics stated that this hammer was most likely used to cause the wounds to the back of his head.

Blood found on the seat and headrest on the driver's side of the car was also Albert's. It was determined that Albert had been hit in the back of the head immediately after pulling into his driveway. He either had a passenger in the back seat of his car or someone was in the back without his knowledge. Multiple sets of prints were found in the car.

Albert had a blood alcohol level of .6, indicating he had been drinking but was not drunk. His cell phone was not found on his person, in his home, or in his car, indicating that the killer had probably taken it with him. A search warrant had been issued for his phone records, in the hopes that they could trace any recent phone calls that Albert had made or received.

A half-empty gas container was found on Albert's patio, along with a lighter that is commonly used to ignite barbeque grills. The police were still trying to determine if these items belonged to Albert.

The coroner determined that, although Albert had been knocked unconscious, he was alive when he was stabbed in the belly button with a scalpel and set on fire.

Further investigation showed that Albert had been drinking with friends at The Lonely Steer. Witnesses said he had not drunk to excess, seemed fine to drive, and was in a good mood when he left the bar. When asked what time Albert left, the witnesses told the investigating officer that it was probably around 12:30 and 1:00.

Detective Myers threw the report on his desk. They had nothing. Albert was alive and well at 12:30 and dead when his neighbor found him an hour later. Myers decided he needed to talk to Wendy Berg and Henry Pullman and find out what the hell happened sixteen years ago.

Wendy Berg was drop-dead gorgeous. Detective Myers forced himself not to stare at her when she invited him into her home. He found that task extremely challenging and tried concentrating on his surroundings.

"You have an absolutely gorgeous home, Ms. Berg," he told her.

"Please, call me Wendy. Have a seat, Detective. Would you care for something to drink? Coffee or a soft drink, perhaps?"

"Is the coffee made? I wouldn't want to bother you if you need to make a fresh pot, but a cup of coffee sounds great."

Wendy turned towards the kitchen door and said," James, would you please bring Detective Myers a cup of coffee?"

Turning back to Myers she asked, "How do you take it? Black or with cream or sugar?"

"Black is fine," Myers replied.

"He takes it black," Wendy said loudly, again turning towards the door.

"I didn't realize you had company," Myers said. "Perhaps this isn't a good time for you."

"It's a perfect time, Detective," she said. "James is my friend. I'm sure you've met before. It's Peter Mont's father, Dr. James Mont."

"Hello, Myers," Dr. Mont said, as he walked into the room, carrying two cups of coffee.

"Doctor," Myers acknowledged him. "Good to see you. I'm a little surprised to see you here," he said, as he took one of the cups from him. "Thanks."

"When Wendy told me you were coming over, we thought it might help if I was here. She's been horribly upset over the deaths of two friends."

"To be honest with you Doctor, I need all the help I can get. We don't have an awful lot to go on right now."

"I don't see how I can possibly help," Wendy said. "It's been years since I talked to Emma. I would occasionally see Albert and we'd talk, but it's probably been five or six months since I last saw him."

"Doctor, I don't mean to upset you, but we have evidence that their deaths may have something to do with the fire that killed your son and Donna Mason. Wendy, I need you to tell me everything that you remember about that night."

"Seriously, Detective? It's taken me sixteen years to try to forget that night. And, I wasn't even there, remember? What do you think I could say now that would make a difference?"

"Hold, on Wendy," Doctor Mont said. "If you can remember something that might help him, then I think you should tell him."

"I wasn't there," she exclaimed. "How many times do I have to tell people that?"

"Do you have any idea what happened that night? Emma told her parents that it was her fault. She mentioned some type of a game they were playing that went bad. Do you know what she meant?" Myers asked her.

"Detective, I'll tell you the same thing I told the police when they talked to me. We invited Donna and Henry to see if they might want to be members of our club. I didn't feel well earlier in the evening and I went home. That's it. I can't tell you anything else, because I don't know anything else."

"I just figured you must have talked to your friends after the fire. They must have told you what happened."

"They told me a candle fell over onto some books and that started the fire. But you already know that."

"Do you have any idea what the game was that they were playing?"

"I have no idea," Wendy replied.

"Why were you considering adding more members to your club? It's my understanding that it was just the six of you for six years. Why did you want to include Donna and Henry after all those years?"

"They were nice. Anyway, we were just considering it. It wasn't a done deal. We asked them to come so we could – you know – interview them."

"So, there's nothing you can think of that would connect that night to Emma's and Albert's deaths?"

"I'm sorry, Detective, but there's not. I wish I could help, but I just don't know anything else."

"Well, then, I guess that's it," Myers said, standing up. "Thanks for the coffee."

"If I think of anything, I'll call you," Wendy told him.

"I'd appreciate it."

As Myers opened the door to leave, he hesitated, turned back to Wendy and Dr. Mont, and asked, "One more thing, Wendy. Who brought the scalpel to the party?"

Wendy's expression did not change. Dr. Mont stood and faced him. "What kind of a question is that? What scalpel are you talking about?"

"A scalpel was found after the fire. You're a

doctor, so Peter would probably have been able to get his hands on one. The emergency room doctor found cuts on Henry's stomach, after the fire. Clean cuts that could have been made with a scalpel. Henry always said he didn't know how he got them, but I think he's lying."

"This is ridiculous," Dr. Mont said.

"Is it, Wendy?" Myers asked. "Is it ridiculous or was that scalpel used to cut Albert?"

Wendy looked up at him. "I told you I wasn't there. Now, if you don't mind, I'd like you to leave."

Fourteen

Sarah Compton had been put on hold for over five minutes. Just as she was about to end the call, Detective Myers came on the line.

"Sorry," he said, breathing hard. "I didn't mean to keep you waiting that long."

Sarah laughed. "Sounds like you need to catch your breath. You a little out of shape there, Detective? Eating too many of those donuts, maybe?"

Myers smiled. Still, the little smart ass that she was years ago, he thought. "Probably just getting old. So, how are you, Sarah?"

"Busy, as usual. Crime never ends, as you well enough know. I must say, though, that I'm a little concerned about what happened to Emma and Albert. I understand you're now calling Emma's death a murder. What made you change your mind?"

"Several things. Too many coincidences between the two deaths."

"One of those coincidences a scalpel?" Sarah asked him.

"It just might be," he replied. "Who you been talking to, Sarah? How do you know so much about these cases?"

"Do you know who I work for, Detective? My

boss talks to your boss, you know."

"Well, if you know what's going on here, then you know that we've decided that these murders are probably connected to that fire sixteen years ago."

"I heard that. It just doesn't make sense to me. Why now, after all these years? And, who could be doing this?"

"You tell me. You know what happened that night. You all do, but nobody's talking. What went on in that treehouse that night, Sarah?"

"What are you looking for, Detective? We told you what happened back then. Nothing has changed."

"I want to know what the game was that you played. I want to know how Henry Pullman got cut. I want to know what the hell happened that was so terrible that Emma Lockhart tried to kill herself a couple of times. I want to know why we found a scalpel after the fire and why we are finding them now at the scenes of these murders. I've got a lot of questions, Sarah, and I'm finding it pretty hard to get any answers."

"Maybe you're overthinking this. Maybe there's just a nut running around town killing people."

"Or, maybe – just maybe – one of your little gang members talked to the wrong person. And, maybe –

just maybe – that person is out to seek revenge for the death of their loved one."

"Then it would have to be someone close to Peter or Donna," Sarah said.

"What can you tell me, Sarah?"

"Let me think about this for a while," she said. "Let me see if I can come up with anything that might help you."

"Don't take too long. I have a feeling that whoever is doing this isn't done yet. There are only four of you left."

"You think I don't know that?" she asked.

"Think hard and fast, Sarah. Just because you don't live in Kalispell doesn't mean you're safe."

"I'll call you soon, Detective," Sarah said and hit the end call button on her phone.

Detective Myers had called Henry Pullman and had asked if it would be okay if he stopped over at his house around 8:00 p.m. He was now sitting in Henry's living room, in an extremely comfortable recliner.

He found Henry Pullman to be extremely friendly and outgoing. Henry was a good-looking man of twenty-eight, although he looked younger. His wife, Jean, was a very pretty woman with dark brown hair and green eyes. She had a superb figure which, Myers was sure, she would maintain after having children.

"Do you know why I asked to talk to you, Henry?" Myers asked.

"I would assume it's about Albert. It's horrible, what happened to him."

"Are you aware that we are now treating Emma's death as a homicide, also?"

Henry gave the detective a blank stare, letting this information sink in. "I thought she killed herself," he finally said.

"That's what we thought at first. Especially, with her history of attempting suicide over the years. However, now with what has happened with Albert – well, there are too many similarities. We're now calling her death a murder."

"I'm sorry to hear that. Do you have any suspects?"

"Everyone's a suspect until we prove them otherwise. But do we have enough to suspect one certain person? The answer is no. We do know, though, that these killings are connected to the fire."

"What fire? You mean Albert being set on fire?"

"No. I mean the fire that happened sixteen years ago, Henry. The one where you lost your friends. The one where you got cut. How did that happen, by the way? How did you get cut? I've never quite figured that one out."

"Quite honestly, Detective, I don't remember. I don't remember much about that night at all. Just what people have told me happened. It's like my mind has blocked it out."

"You don't remember anything?"

"Not a thing. Is there anything else I can do for you?"

Myers looked at him, trying to decide if he was lying or really did not remember that night. Another dead end, he thought. He thanked Henry and Jean and left their home.

Myers sat in his car, thinking about his next step. He was getting nowhere. He took out his phone and looked up a number, called it, and waited. A woman answered on the second ring.

"Hello."

"Mrs. Pullman, this is Detective Myers with the Kalispell Police Department. I was wondering if you could answer a question for me."

"Oh, my. Did something happen?"

"Nothing to worry about. Nothing's wrong. I was

just wondering if you could tell me how Henry got cut during that fire."

"Detective, are you talking about the treehouse fire?"

"Yes, ma'am."

"That was horrible, wasn't it?"

"Yes, ma'am, it certainly was."

"I'm sorry, but I can't help you. Henry doesn't remember anything about that night. It's like he got amnesia about it. His mind just seemed to block it out."

"I see. Nothing at all?"

"Nothing. Well, he probably remembers what we told him about it. But he has no memories of his own about that night."

"Thank you, Mrs. Pullman."

"May I ask why you're asking me about this now?"

"It's nothing important. We're just checking out a few things and the subject came up. Thank you, again."

"Night, Detective."

Fifteen

Almost a month had passed since Albert's death. Detective Myers was stumped. The forensic evidence that had been collected at Albert's home made it clear what had happened, but not by whom. Myers was kicking himself for not treating Emma's death as a murder from the beginning. Most likely there was evidence they had overlooked because they thought her death was a suicide.

Myers had contacted the Lockharts on a number of occasions to keep them updated on his findings. He had asked for Emma's phone, so he could trace the call she had received the night she was killed. That had led nowhere. The call had come from a burner phone.

He had talked to everyone, still living, that had been in the treehouse the night of the fire. He had talked to all the parents. No one knew anything or, if they did, they weren't talking.

He had two unsolved murders on his hands. If he didn't get a break soon, he had a feeling that these were going to wind up being cold cases. Not on my watch, he thought, as he leaned forward in his chair to answer the phone.

"Myers," he answered.

"This is Mike Simpson, from Universal Medical Supply. I'm sorry it took so long for me to get back to you, Detective. I've been out of the office for a couple of weeks."

"Yes, Mike. I was wondering if I was going to hear back from you. Have you found out anything?"

"Not really. There's one thing that seems a little off, but I'm reaching here. A Dr. James Mont ordered a single box of scalpels from us a few months back. Do you know him?"

"Yes, I do. Why would that be unusual? He is a doctor."

"First of all, there's no reason for him to be ordering them. If he needs a scalpel for surgery, it's provided by the hospital. By the way, when the hospital places an order, it's for a lot more than just a single box."

"How many are in a box?" Myers asked him.

"Ten. He ordered one box of Miltex Disposable Scalpels and had the order sent to his office."

"And, this is unusual for a doctor to do?"

"It unusual for anyone to order just one box," Mike replied. "However, seeing as how he is a doctor, we sent the order out."

"What was the date of the order?"

"June 30th. He probably got them a few days later."

"Is this the first time he's had medical supplies shipped to his office?"

"Oh, no. We send a wide variety of items to him all the time. You know - supplies that a doctor would need in his office. But, it's the first time he ordered scalpels."

"That's it then?"

"That's all I've got for you. I hope it helps you catch the son of a bitch that did this."

"So do I, Mike. Thanks a lot."

"Bye."

Myers decided a face-to-face with Dr. Mont would be better than calling him. He called Mont's office and asked the receptionist if the doctor was seeing patients today. He was told that he would be there from 1:00 to 6:00. Myers decided to be Mont's first appointment of the day. He glanced at his watch and saw that it was already 11:30. Just enough time to grab some lunch and head over to Mont's office, Myers thought and left the building.

Myers smiled to himself when he entered Dr.

Mont's office and saw Mont's expression. It definitely was not a happy one. Although Mont's receptionist told Myers that her boss was busy, Myers walked into his office before she had a chance to stop him.

"Detective Myers," Mont said. "I didn't know you had an appointment."

"I don't. I have a few questions for you."

"I have patients waiting and I don't have time right now. Perhaps, you could come back later today. Let's say around 6:30 or 7:00."

"Let's not. I'm here now and this is only going to take a few minutes. I would like to know why you ordered scalpels from Universal Medical Supplies."

Dr. Mont grinned. "I'm a doctor. I order scalpels all the time. What's so unusual about it?"

"No, Doctor, you don't. You may order medical supplies for your office, but not scalpels. Last June you ordered one box of scalpels. That's a first. May I ask why?"

"Of course. There are certain procedures that I do in my office that require that instrument."

"For instance?"

"Well, let's see. I may have to lance a boil. Occasionally I remove a mole or a growth to have it biopsied. I do quite a few simple procedures that do not require going to the hospital."

"You've been doing this for a while? In your office, I mean. Or, is this something you just started?"

"For years, Detective. It's nothing new."

"Then, how come you just recently started buying scalpels? There's no record of you purchasing any before June 30th."

"There are several reasons. I used to take a box or two from the hospital. Oh, I'd pay for them. I wasn't stealing. Then, after the hospital put an end to it, I started getting them on Amazon, but the quality wasn't that good. So, I decided to give Universal a try. The end of June was the first time I placed an order with them. I only ordered one box because I wanted to check out their quality before I bought in quantity."

"I see. Do you have any left?"

"I'm sure I do. I don't use that many."

"May I see them, Doctor?" Myers asked.

"You want to see them? I'm not sure where they are."

"Then I suggest you find out."

"They are probably in different exam rooms. I'm not sure which ones."

"Well, let's find out, shall we? Call Gladys – that was her name, wasn't it? Call her in here."

Dr. Mont sat back in his big leather chair and gave Myers a dirty look. "I'm busy, Detective. This will have to wait."

Myers sighed. "Do I really have to get a search warrant, Doctor? Just call her in here and let's get this settled now."

Mont glared at Myers for a couple of seconds, hit the intercom button, and asked Gladys to come into his office. She opened the door and asked what he needed.

"Gladys, do you know where the scalpels are kept?" Dr. Mont asked.

She smiled at him. "Well, of course, I do. We keep them in the cabinet in the lab."

Myers gave her his best smile, and said, "Would you be so kind as to get them for us? Are all the scalpels kept there, or are there some in the exam rooms?"

"Oh, no, Detective. There aren't any in the exam rooms. Just the lab."

"I see."

"Do you still want me to get them?" Gladys asked.

"Please."

As Gladys left the office, Myers turned and gave

the doctor a questioning look. "All over the place, huh?"

Dr. Mont shrugged. "What do I know? I only work here. Gladys runs the place."

Gladys was still smiling as she walked back into the office, carrying a small box. "Who should I give it to?" she inquired.

"I'll take it," said Myers, as he took the box from her and laid it on the desk.

He opened it, reached inside, and pulled out eight individually wrapped scalpels. He looked up at Gladys and asked, "These come ten to a box, right?"

Detective Myers had asked Dr. Mont to accompany him to the police station. Dr. Mont had immediately picked up his phone and called his attorney, requesting that he meet them there.

Now, four men were seated at a small table in an interrogation room in the police station. There were no windows, it was hot and stuffy and the bright, irritating fluorescent lights bothered everyone's eyes.

"Is my client under arrest?" Samuel Mason asked.

"No," Detective Henry replied. "He hasn't been charged with anything. We simply need to ask him a few questions."

"Couldn't you have asked these questions when you were at his office, Morris?" Mason asked the detective.

"I tried," Myers said. "He got a little hostile with me. It seemed like a better idea to question him here, where he would be less likely to take another swing at me."

"Dr. Mont hit you?" the lawyer asked Myers.

"He tried."

Dr. Mont looked at Myers. "Can you please turn the air conditioner on? It's like an oven in here," he said. "And, turn some of these lights off. They're killing my eyes."

"Sorry, Doctor," Myers said. "We can't control the temperature from in here."

"Well, then, at least turn some of those lights off," Mont said.

"Detective Henry, you want to turn some of those lights off?" Myers asked.

"Can't. They're all on one switch," Detective Henry said.

"Is that a fact? Sorry, Doctor, looks like all of the lights stay on," Myers told him.

"Detective, just what is it you want from my

client? He needs to get back to his patients."

"I need him to tell us where the two missing scalpels are."

Dr. Mont looked at his attorney, who was sitting next to him. "Do I have to answer any of his damn questions, Samuel? I'm not under arrest. I haven't done anything wrong, and I need to get the hell out of here."

"I could arrest you if that's what it will take to get you to cooperate," Myers said.

"Dr. Mont, just answer that question and you can leave," said Detective Henry. "We're just trying to account for two scalpels that are missing from your office."

"They're not missing, you idiot," Mont yelled. "I used them and they were properly discarded."

"Easy, James," his lawyer said. "Don't get all riled up. The detectives are just doing their job."

"Go call Gladys. She can tell you when those scalpels were used and why," said Mont.

"Detective, do you mind if I call her and ask her about this?" the lawyer asked.

"Be our guest. Just get an answer from her so we can figure out if we are going to arrest your client for murder or let him leave," replied Myers.

"Well, for a little while I thought you had your guy," Detective Kyle Henry said to Myers.

"So did I. Especially when we found out that the brand of the scalpels he bought and the ones left at the crime scenes were the same. I just can't get a break on these murders, Henry."

"Do you trust that Gladys was telling the truth?"

"Well, he is her boss. Maybe she would cover for him," Myers said.

"You don't really think Dr. Mont killed those two, do you, Myers?"

"I honestly don't know. His son was burned alive in that fire. If anyone would want revenge, it would be him."

"Hopefully, something will pop soon," said Detective Henry. "Give it some time."

"Time is all I've got right now," said Myers. "I need a hell of a lot more than time to solve these cases."

Sixteen

Every year since Brad Weiss had opened his bar, he had held an "end of summer" party for his staff. He hired outsiders to work the bar and serve the food, as he wanted to be sure his employees were free to drink, eat, and swim in his pool. Badminton and croquet games were set up for those who wanted to play lawn games. The guest pool house was available to couples who wanted a little privacy.

Brad always held the parties on Sunday, so his staff had Monday to recuperate. There were a few who went home sober, but the majority of his employees kept the cab companies busy on those Sunday nights.

Brad was sitting in an oversized padded lawn chair, under an umbrella, observing his guests. He had a large staff and, except for a few, they were all single. The married ones brought their spouses, but absolutely no children were allowed. Almost everyone was topless and, in some cases, totally nude.

Brad wondered if he would ever get tired of looking at nude women. Twelve fantastic young women danced at his bar. Three of these dancers took turns spending nights with him. Occasionally, he would enjoy all of them on the same night and at the same time.

He also had six bartenders, eight waitresses, and a couple of bouncers working for him. At the present time, he had thirty people on his payroll, including the cleanup crew. He had little turnover as the money was great, he offered fantastic benefits, and a yearly bonus.

Today was the day he paid out the yearly bonuses. He didn't go along with the traditional custom of giving Christmas bonuses. He figured his staff could use their bonuses more this time of year. He gave them all a turkey the week before Christmas, but nothing else.

In a few hours, Brad would hand out over $100,000.00 in bonuses to his employees. Some of them would get more than others, depending on how long they had been with him. His three girl toys would get the most.

Because Brad had made it clear that he didn't want gifts at Christmas, his staff had started the tradition of giving him gifts at his annual "end of summer" party. For the first few years, Brad had tried to discourage them from doing this, but now he looked forward to it.

He glanced over at the table holding the gifts. He knew that none of them had cost much and that a lot of them would be sex-oriented. He smiled. He was happy with his life. He was content with what he had. He was rich – oh, so rich. Yes, he thought, life is good.

He noticed a card laying on the edge of the gift table, about to fall. He reached over and grabbed it. The outside of the envelope was blank. He opened it and pulled out a card, and smiled. On the front of the card was a picture of an extremely large-breasted woman. He opened the card, read the inside, and quickly closed it. Brad glanced around to see if anyone was watching him and realized his hands were shaking.

Shit, he thought, this isn't funny. Who the hell could have put that card there? The only people he didn't know personally were the caterers he had hired to work the party. Was it one of them, he wondered.

He needed to call Sarah. He left his chair, walked into his house, and called her number.

"Hey, Brad," she answered. "What can I do for you on this fine Sunday afternoon?"

"Listen to this. 'My wounds do not heal; the fire burns bright. Someone will die by my hands tonight. You cannot hide, there's no place to go. And when you burn, I hope you burn slow.' Did you hear that, Sarah? Did you?" he yelled.

"Brad, slow down. Why did you say that to me?"

"I just received this card. That was written on the inside of the card. What do you think I should do?" Brad asked her.

"Okay. Settle down. Read it to me one more time."

"My wounds do not heal; the fire burns bright. Someone will die by my hands tonight. You cannot hide, there's no place to go. And when you burn, I hope you burn slow."

"When did you get the card?"

"It's my annual pool party. It was on the gift table. I don't know who put it there."

"Don't let anyone leave. I'm calling the police. You better hide the drugs and get some clothes on those people."

"I know everyone here except the people working the party."

"Don't let anyone leave. You understand?"

"I understand. What about you? Are you safe?" Brad asked.

"I'm coming over as soon as I call the police. I'm also calling Detective Myers."

"From Kalispell? What can he do? He's hours away."

"He needs to know there's been a threat. Now get off the phone and make sure no one leaves."

The guests had been allowed to leave shortly after the police arrived. Brad apologized to them and told them that there would be a repeat party the following Sunday.

The people working the party were questioned and, after the police found nothing suspicious, were told they could also leave the party.

Now, four hours later, Sarah and Brad were sitting by the pool, talking and having a drink.

"It's obvious that someone wants to kill us," said Brad. "I'm not ready to die. I'm seriously thinking about taking a long vacation. Maybe Alaska. I wouldn't mind getting out of this heat for a while."

"Maybe I'll go with you," Sarah replied, smiling. "I think it's time we told the police what happened that night, Brad. It really was an accident and we were only twelve. It's not like we wanted to kill anyone. We were just playing a game."

"A game that got two of our friends killed, remember? None of it would have happened if we hadn't tried to scare Donna and Henry. It's all Emma's fault for ever suggesting it."

"No, Brad," said Sarah, "we're all at fault. We were bored kids trying to have some fun at Donna's and Henry's expense. We made them think we were going to let them join our club when we knew we weren't. We were dumb stupid kids. But now people are dying because of something that happened sixteen years ago. I think we need to tell the police. Maybe, then, they can figure out who is doing this."

"Now I'm the target. You read that card. He's going to kill me next."

"How do you even know it's a he?" Sarah asked.

Brad gave her a questioning look. "You're right," he said. "It could be anyone."

"Yes, anyone."

"So, what do we do now?" Brad asked.

"Keep your doors locked and keep looking over your shoulder."

"You have a gun, Sarah? I can give you one if you want."

"Thanks, but I have a real nice 45. I'm set."

"You a good shot?"

"Pretty good, I guess."

"How about I get you a real nice sawed-off shotgun? You just point it and pull the trigger."

Sarah thought about it for a few seconds. "I

think I'd like that, Brad. Thanks."

Seventeen

At two o'clock the next morning, the Helena Fire Department received a call that there had been an explosion out on Evergreen Drive. It took them seventeen minutes to arrive at the scene. Brad Weiss' one-and-a-half million-dollar home had been destroyed. Except for the unattached guest house and horse stable, nothing was left standing. Debris, some still burning when the fire department arrived, was scattered all over the property. The fireman put out the small fires and started combing the area for bodies or body parts. None were found.

When Detective Stanley West tried to contact Brad Weiss to inform him of the explosion and the loss of his home, his call immediately went to voice mail.

When Sarah Compton arrived at work Monday morning, she heard the news of the explosion for the first time. She knocked on her boss' door and asked if she could speak to him. A half-hour later she left the building, went home, packed a few items in an overnight bag, and drove out of town, headed to Kalispell. It was time to talk to Detective Myers and tell him the truth about what had transpired on July 13, 1999.

As Sarah drove out of Helena, Brad Weiss deplaned in Anchorage, Alaska. He figured a week or two away from home, going fishing, and just relaxing was what he needed right now. Some crazy asshole was going to try to kill him and he figured he didn't need to make it easy for him. He doubted that whoever had left the note would follow him to Alaska. Only Sarah knew where he was. I should have insisted that she come with me, he thought. If I'm not around she may be the next one on this crazy-ass person's list.

He turned on his phone and noticed that he had numerous voice messages. He put the phone back in his pocket, deciding he could listen to them after he got settled into his room at the lodge.

"Come in, Detective," Martha Compton said, as she answered the door. "Sarah called and said you were meeting her here around 3:30. She seems to be running late. I expected her to be here a couple of hours ago."

"Perhaps she had car trouble," Myers said. "Have you tried calling her?"

"Oh, no. I would never call her while I know she's driving a car. It's too dangerous, you know.

Driving and talking on the phone at the same time."

"Let me try her," Myers said. "Maybe she'll pick up and we can find out why she's running late."

"Well, I guess just once would be okay. You are a policeman, so you should know what's best," replied Mrs. Compton.

"Do you have her number handy?" Myers asked her.

As Sarah's mother recited the phone number, Detective Myers called and waited for Sarah to pick up. There was no response.

"I can't imagine what has happened to her," Mrs. Compton said.

When he heard a phone ringing, Detective Myers turned towards the kitchen. He heard a man talking and turned back to Mrs. Compton. "Is that your husband in the kitchen?" he asked.

"Yes. He's having lunch. He works a swing shift, so this is his lunch time. Rather late, I know. But, when you work strange hours you eat at strange times," she replied.

"It sounds like he's on the phone. Perhaps you should check to see if that's Sarah calling him," Myers said.

Mrs. Compton shook her head in agreement and

walked into the kitchen. Her husband was sitting in a chair with his head in his hands. "What is it, John? Who called?"

John Compton looked up at his wife, tears streaming down his face. "It's Sarah, Martha. She's dead. Someone killed our little girl."

Martha Compton stared at her husband for a brief moment and then collapsed onto the kitchen floor.

If it hadn't been for the black smoke filling the sky, Sarah probably wouldn't have been found so soon. At around 11:00 a.m. an elderly couple, driving north on MT 83, pulled over to the side of the road and called the State Patrol. They informed them that something was burning a few miles in from the highway, which could possibly be a forest fire.

A State Patrolman arrived about twenty minutes later and talked to the couple. They pointed out where the smoke had been but told the policeman that it wasn't as dense as it had been when they had first called. The patrolman thanked them, informed the couple he would check it out, and told them it was okay for them to continue on their way.

The patrolman then drove down a narrow, dirt

road, which was overgrown with weeds, and discovered Sarah's car burning. He grabbed the fire extinguisher that he carried in his squad car and put out the fire. He then called the Helena Police Department and told them to send out a forensic team and the coroner.

As soon as he had a preliminary report from the coroner, Detective Stanley West called Detective Myers in Kalispell.

"What happened, Stan? Do you have anything yet?"

"Well, we figure it's all connected. Someone blew up Brad Weiss' house early this morning. Now we . . . "

"Somebody tried to Kill Brad? I hadn't heard about that. Sarah Compton called me yesterday and asked if we could meet. She said that Brad had received a threatening note," Myers interrupted.

"We can't find Brad. We've got an APB out for him. So, Sarah was on her way to Kalispell to meet with you?"

"Ya. We were supposed to meet around 3:30 at her parent's house. She wanted to tell me something regarding a couple of murders we've had here in the past few months."

"Well, it looks like somebody ran her off the

road. Her car has a few dents in it. We haven't figured out why she left the highway and drove down an old dirt road. Maybe she didn't do it voluntarily. Maybe there were two people and one held a gun to her head and made her drive there. We just don't know yet. The rest is bad, Myers. Really bad. We don't know exactly how she died."

"The fire didn't kill her?" Myers asked.

"Well, maybe it did. There's no way to know until we get the coroner's report. She had multiple stab wounds and the ground near the car is soaked with her blood. If she had smoke in her lungs, then we'll know she was alive when the car was set on fire."

"What's multiple?"

"Shit. Perhaps as many as twenty. Maybe more."

"Sounds like overkill to me," said Myers.

"They gutted her, Morris. They stabbed her over and over and then gutted her. Then they threw her in the car, like a sack of garbage, and set the car on fire."

"You keep saying they? You pretty sure it was more than one person?"

"The coroner is pretty sure that more than one knife was used. Two knives usually mean two people."

"What kind of knives? Can he tell?"

"He knows that one had a jagged edge. He can

tell that from some of the cuts. The other cuts are clean cuts and not as deep."

"Could they have come from a scalpel?" Myers asked.

"I guess so. Hell, I don't know. The coroner just started his exam. We'll know more later on today or tomorrow."

"I don't get it, Stan. How the hell can the coroner tell all this if her body was burned?" Myers asked.

"Her body wasn't burned that badly. Most of the fire was contained to the back seat and it was more smoke than fire. We don't think an accelerate was used to start the fire. Just some paper and a match. It was like they were in a big hurry to get the hell out of there."

"There's no doubt that it's Sarah?"

"No doubt. The patrolman recognized her immediately. Seeing as how she worked in the DA's office, she was well known by law enforcement. Plus, her purse was intact and on the floor of the front seat. It had her driver's license in it."

"I was with her parents when they got the phone call from State Patrol. I had to call an ambulance for her mom," said Myers.

"I believe it. I tried to talk to the father, but he

was so devastated he could hardly put a sentence together. Anyway, the coroner won't be able to release the body for a few days. This is a big deal here, Myers. Sarah had a great future ahead of her. She was well-known and well-liked. There's going to be hell around here if we don't solve this one fast."

"Where do you think Brad Weiss is?" Myers asked.

"I think he took that note seriously and left town. I only wish Sarah had done the same thing."

"So, do I. I really liked her. Let me know what else you find out. I'm going to start working the case here and see if I can find out who was out of town yesterday and today."

"Send me what you have on the other two murders. We've got to stay tight on this. By the way, how many kids belonged to that treehouse club?" West asked.

"There were six. Donna Mason and Henry Pullman were not part of the group but were there that night. Five of the eight are now dead."

"Well, Myers, let's hope we find the bastard or bastards who are doing this before another one is killed."

"One more thing," Myers said.

"What's that?"

"Are you sure there wasn't a scalpel laying around there someplace? It seems to be the killer's calling card."

"We went over the whole area. We didn't find anything. We do have tire tracks, but you know the chances of matching them to a vehicle. Slim and none."

"Thanks. I'll talk to you later, Stan," Myers said.

"Over and out," said Detective Stan West and hung up the phone.

Eighteen

Wendy Berg told Detective Myers she had been with Dr. Mont when Brad's house was blown up. Dr. Mont confirmed that they had been together. On Monday morning, Wendy was working at her job as an accountant for the Lullaby Crib Company. Wendy was in the clear.

Henry Pullman's wife verified that Henry had been in town both Sunday and Monday. Henry's manager told Myers that Henry had been on the floor selling cars by 9:00 on Monday morning. Myers figured he could rule him out as a suspect.

Myers had asked a few of his police officers to follow up with the victims' parents regarding their whereabouts on Sunday and Monday. Myers had already talked to Mont, so didn't feel the need to talk to him again. He had decided he should be the one to talk to the Lockharts and was now in their living room, discussing Emma's murder.

"I was wondering if you remembered anything else that Emma might have said," he said to Emma's parents.

"We have racked our brains," said Arthur Lockhart. "Nothing. We have nothing. You must remember, Detective, that Emma rarely left the house.

She basically had no life, much less a social one. She received an occasional phone call, but they were few and far between."

"You still don't have any idea who may have called her that night?" Myers asked.

"We don't," said Caroline Lockhart. "I'm sorry we can't help you."

"An attempt was made on Brad Weiss' life early yesterday morning. Fortunately, he wasn't at home when it happened."

"Oh, my God," said Mrs. Lockhart. "Is he okay?"

"He's fine. Sarah Compton wasn't quite so lucky, however. She was found dead yesterday morning. She was murdered," Myers told them.

He watched their expressions as he gave them the news. Mrs. Lockhart started sobbing when she heard about Sarah. Mr. Lockhart got a blank look on his face, started to tear up, stood, and left the room.

They didn't know, Myers thought. They are truly upset. This is a shock to them.

Myers gave them a few minutes to compose themselves. Arthur Lockhart came back into the room and sat next to his wife. He looked at Myers, tears in his eyes, and said, "Is there anything we can do? How are Sarah's parents doing?"

"Her mother is in the hospital. She collapsed when she heard the news."

"So, tell me, Detective, how many more are going to die?" Mr. Lockhart yelled, suddenly getting upset. "What are you doing to catch this maniac? Why aren't you out there doing something? Go do your job . . . "

"Arthur. Stop," Caroline Lockhart cried. "He is doing his job. Yelling isn't going to help anything."

"I'll damn well yell if I want to. Three children have been killed in the past few months and no one can tell us what's going on."

Mrs. Lockhart took her husband's hand. "Yes, Arthur. I know. And, I'm sure that Detective Myers is doing his best to find out who's doing this."

Myers waited a few seconds, watching the anger leave Mr. Lockhart's face. Then he sighed, looked at them, and said, "I'm sorry to ask you this. Very sorry. But I have to ask you where you were Sunday and Monday."

Arthur Lockhart looked like he was ready to kill Myers. "You son of a bitch," he yelled. "Get the hell out of my house."

"I'm leaving as soon as you tell me where you and your wife were on Sunday and Monday."

"We were in town, Detective," answered Caroline

Lockhart, in a soft voice. "On Sunday we went to church like we always do. Arthur stayed after and helped count the collection. I came home and fixed dinner."

"Caroline, stop," said Arthur. "You don't need to tell him where we were. It's none. . . "

"We spent the rest of the day here," Caroline continued. "On Monday I packed a lunch and we went to the cemetery and we spent most of the day with Emma. We do that every Monday, Detective. Emma died on a Monday, so we spend time with her on Mondays."

"Now are you satisfied?" Arthur Lockhart asked Myers. "Happy now?"

"Arthur, I'm sorry I had to question you. It's part of my job. And, no, this doesn't make me happy. Please believe me when I say that nothing is more important to me, right now, than catching the psycho who is doing this."

"We know, Detective. We're still on edge, I guess," said Caroline Lockhart. "Please keep in touch."

"One more thing," Myers said, as he walked to the door. "Have you gone through Emma's things yet?"

"I'm still working on it," said Caroline.

Two hours later, Myers had completed his detailed police reports. He had talked to Wendy Berg, Dr. James Mont, Henry Pullman, and the Lockharts. Something was off, he thought. He read through what he had written in his reports once more.

He sat back, thinking hard. Something isn't adding up and I can't put my finger on it. He laid the papers back on his desk. It will come to me, he thought. It always does.

He picked up the police reports his men had written after they had questioned the rest of the parents. The officers had talked to John and Patricia Freeman, John and Martha Compton, Cole and Barbara Mason, and David and Alice Weiss. He skimmed them, looking for something to pop out. Nothing. Then, he carefully read each one of the short reports.

Everyone was accounted for when Brad's house was blown to pieces. Everyone had an alibi for the time that Sarah was forced off the highway and murdered.

He had nothing.

Nineteen

Brad Weiss laid his phone on the table and stared out the window. The view overlooking the lake, with the Chugach Mountain Range's snow-capped mountains glistening in the background, was breathtaking. He jumped as a waiter asked him if he would care for more coffee.

"Sorry," he said. "Guess I was in another world. Just the check, please."

Sarah was dead and his house was gone – blown to smithereens – by some fucker who was trying to wipe out everyone who had been in the treehouse that night. Why now, he wondered. And, who? It had to be someone who wanted revenge for either Donna's or Peter's death.

He couldn't believe what had been done to Sarah. She must have suffered terribly, he thought. Detective Myers had told him there was no doubt it was the same person that had killed Emma and Albert.

Brad went back to his room and packed up his clothes. He was going home. He had talked to his manager at his bar and told him to keep an eye on things, and that he would be back later in the week. Right now, he had a plane to catch to Kalispell, where

Detective Myers would be waiting for him. They had a lot to talk about.

Detective Myers hoped he was finally going to get some answers. He had talked to Brad Weiss, after finally tracking him down in Anchorage, and Brad had agreed to meet with him.

Myers felt a little sorry for the young man. He had lost another friend plus his home. Brad's reaction to what had happened to Sarah had been interesting, to say the least. Brad wasn't surprised that she was dead. He told Meyers that he had wanted her to come with him, but she had refused.

Brad was surprised, though, at his home being blown up. Myers laughed to himself. Surprised certainly is not the right word, he thought. The air must have turned blue when Brad found out his home was gone. The man's no dummy, though, Myers thought. He was smart enough to get out of town after he got that threatening note. He took it seriously, especially after what happened to his friends. Too bad Sarah hadn't listened to him.

Myers checked his watch. Brad's flight would be leaving in a couple of hours. He should be in Kalispell around six.

Brad had called Detective Myers from the airport to tell him that his flight had just arrived and he needed a drink. He suggested they meet at The Lonely Steer Bar.

Myers immediately drove to the bar and secured a booth in the back, assuring they would have privacy. He ordered a scotch on the rocks and waited for Brad to arrive.

Now, Detective Myers was quiet as he focused on what Brad Weiss was telling him. He occasionally picked up his drink and took a sip, but for almost fifteen minutes he hadn't said a word.

Brad was now finishing his second drink and starting to relax a little. Myers didn't blame him for being a nervous wreck. Three of his friends had been brutally murdered and he had been threatened with the same fate.

Brad suddenly stopped talking and looked at Myers.

"What?" Myers asked.

"You want another drink?"

"I'm fine. Are you driving?" Myers asked.

"No. I'm staying at my parent's home tonight. I figure I'll take a taxi or you can drop me off later."

"No problem. I'll give you a ride."

"Well, I'm having one more." Brad glanced around, saw their waitress, and signaled her to bring him another drink.

"What happened next?" Myers asked.

"Total chaos. The place filled up with smoke fast and it was hard to see. Everyone was screaming. Albert tried to get everyone to help put the fire out. At first, he was more concerned about saving the treehouse than anything else. Then, later, he wanted to go back inside and help Donna and Peter. It was too late. We were just kids. It was an accident. We certainly never meant for anyone to get hurt."

"And, you never told anyone about the game?"

"Hell, no. We made a pact to keep it a secret until we died."

"When?" Myers asked.

"When what?" Brad replied.

"When did you make the pact? You all told the same story at the hospital that night."

"The minute Albert hit the ground and we realized that Donna and Peter weren't gonna make it. I don't think anyone ever told Henry that we were playing a game on him and Donna or that we never were going to let them join our club. We swore we would never tell anyone about that dumb autopsy game. Emma made it up, you know. It was her idea. That's why she was never the same. She blamed herself. But, all of us were at fault. Except for Wendy, of course."

"Why not Wendy? Why wasn't she there?" Myers asked.

"She got pissed because we never actually planned on letting Donna and Henry join our club. When she found out we were pranking them and hadn't told her, she got mad and went home." Brad looked down at his drink, the pain of remembering that night on his face. "We were so scared. Even Henry, who didn't do anything wrong. We figured if we told what had happened, we would go to jail."

Myers watched as Brad put his hands to his face, trying to hold back the tears. Brad took a deep breath and looked up at Myers. "And, now I'm more than scared. I'm terrified, wondering if I'm next."

"I don't blame you. Your house was blown up. You'd be dead right now if you hadn't taken that threat seriously."

"Does anything I've told you help?" Brad asked him.

"It does," Myers said. "One of you talked. I'm pretty sure it wasn't you or Sarah. Emma didn't have much contact with anyone, and her parents have alibis. So do Wendy and Henry. My problem here, Brad, is that it doesn't necessarily have to be one of you kids. If any of the parents found out, it could be one of them looking for revenge. It kind of narrows it down to Peter's dad or Donna's parents. We've checked their alibis, but I'm going to check them again."

"In the meanwhile, three of us are still targets. I'd go right back to Alaska, except I've got to get back to Helena and get that mess straightened out. My insurance guy is probably going crazy right now."

"When are you going back home?" Myers asked.

"Tomorrow. Except, I don't have a home anymore."

"Can you stay around one more day? It's late and I've got an early morning. I'd like to go over this with you one more time."

"I guess. It'll be nice to spend some time with mom and dad. I haven't seen them for a while. But, I'm out of here on Friday for sure."

"I appreciate it. Come on. Let's go. It's late and way past my bedtime."

After Myers dropped Brad off at his parent's house, Brad spent an hour catching up with his parents. They finally called it a night around 11:30 and Brad went to his old room. He opened his suitcase and took out his address book. He looked up Henry's phone number and called him. The phone was answered on the third ring.

"Jean, this is Brad Weiss. Is Henry there?"

"Do you have any idea what time it is?" Jean asked.

"Don't care. I want to talk to Henry."

"He's asleep. Call back tomorrow."

"You either wake him and give him that damn phone or I'm coming over there."

"Shit, Brad, you're still a pain in the ass. Hold on."

A few moments went by while Brad listened to Jean waking Henry and telling him that his old asshole friend wanted to talk to him.

"What the fuck, Brad? What's so important that it couldn't wait until tomorrow?" Henry said as he came on the line.

"I'm in town and I want to meet for breakfast. We have a lot to talk about. I'm gonna call and see if Wendy will join us."

"Just the three of us?"

"Yes. Meet me at Swenson's Diner at 8:00."

"I'm off work tomorrow. Jean and I have plans."

"Seriously, Henry? I don't care about your plans. Meet me at 8:00."

"Hold on."

Brad listened once again while Henry and Jean argued about Henry meeting Brad. He laughed at their conversation, glad he wasn't married and henpecked.

"Brad? You still there?"

"So, what did the boss decide? Are you gonna be there?"

"I'll be there at 8:00. But I can't stay long."

"Great. Don't be late," said Brad, and ended the call.

It took Brad almost twenty minutes to convince Wendy to meet him and Henry the next morning at Swenson's Diner. The first few minutes he listened to her yell at him for waking her up, for being an asshole, and that he was just as rude and inconsiderate as he had always been. He let her vent and, when she finally simmered down, he told her why he was calling.

"You're in town? Why didn't you tell me that to start with?" Wendy asked.

"I would have if you had let me get a word in," Brad replied.

"Well, it's late and I was in the middle of

something."

"Got company, do you?" Brad teased.

"None of your stinking business."

"So, will you come? I really think we need to talk."

"I agree. Yes, I'll be there," Wendy said. "I can go in to work a little late. No problem."

"See you at 8:00 then?"

"See you then," Wendy replied, and Brad's phone went dead.

Twenty

By 8:00 the next morning, the three friends were seated and having their first cup of coffee. Wendy, looking as gorgeous as ever, yawned.

"Didn't get much sleep last night?" Brad said, teasingly.

"No. Thanks to you," she replied.

"Oh, I doubt very much it was my fault. I have to say, though, Wendy, you would never tell it by looking at you. You look well-rested and as beautiful as ever."

Wendy laughed. "Watch it, Big Boy. Flattery will get you everywhere."

"I've been waiting for years to hear you say that."

"Dream on," she replied.

"Will you two knock it off," Henry said. "I've got plans with Jean. What's so important you had to wake me in the middle of the night, anyway?"

"Don't you think that three of our friends being murdered is important? I'd be dead right along with them if I hadn't left town."

"I heard about that. It's terrible – someone trying to blow you up. You were lucky," Wendy said.

"Have either of you received any threatening notes?" Brad asked.

"I didn't get any," said Henry.

"Me either," replied Wendy.

"So, obviously I was next on the list," Henry stated. "There's one thing I don't understand, though. Why try to blow me up? The other killings were close up and personal and, if the killer had succeeded in killing me, I'd be in pieces right now. Not stabbed in the gut and set on fire, like the others. Something doesn't add up," said Brad.

"Are we sure it's the same person doing all this?" asked Wendy. "After all, we live hours away from each other. It seems everyone has an alibi for the times of the murders."

"The police are sure it's the same person or persons. It could be more than one. They figure that two people were involved in Sarah's death. Two different knives were used, and one of them was a scalpel, just like with Albert and Emma."

"How do you know that?" Henry asked.

"I talked to Detective Myers last night. He mentioned it to me."

Henry gave Brad a questioning look and asked, "What else did he tell you? More important, Brad – what did you tell him?"

"Everything. I told him the whole story."

"Dear Lord, why would you do that?" asked

Wendy. "We promised never to tell."

"Let me ask you, Wendy. Who have you told? Are you going to sit there and tell me that for the past sixteen years you never told anyone? You, too, Henry. You're married. Husbands and wives tell each other everything. Are you going to tell me that you've never told Jean about what happened the night of the fire?"

"Never," Henry said, too loudly. "I don't remember. That's what I tell people. That's what I've said from the beginning. I don't remember a thing. The doctors call it selective amnesia. I've denied knowing anything for so long that I almost believe it myself. So, no, Brad. I've never said a word to anyone."

"Seriously? How about you, Wendy? You ever tell?"

Wendy looked at the two of them, pursed her lips together, and then smiled. "Well, I did tell someone. But, you know, I thought he had a right to know. After all, his son died that night, and he needed closure. But it was a long time ago."

"You told Dr. Mont, Peter's father?" Henry asked.

"I did, but he promised he would never say anything to anyone about it."

"Are you still dating him?" Henry asked.

Brad turned and looked at Wendy. "I heard that

you were dating him. My god, Wendy, what's wrong with you? He's your father's age." When Brad saw the hurt look on Wendy's face, he said, "I'm sorry. That was out of line. When did you tell him?"

"I don't know," Wendy replied. "A while back. Maybe in May or June."

"That's not a long time ago, Wendy. That's a couple of months ago. And, right before the murders started," said Henry.

"Don't be silly. He's a doctor. He wouldn't hurt anyone." Tears started to fill her eyes. "You can't possibly think that the man I love did this."

"You love? That's crazy," said Brad.

"No, it's not. And, he loves me, too."

"Did it ever occur to you that he started dating you to get information out of you?"

"Now that's crazy. I've been friends with him since I was young. Both, him and his wife. After Mrs. Mont died, one thing led to another and it just took off from there."

"Did you tell Detective Myers you are dating him?" Brad asked her.

"He knows. The whole damn town knows."

"So, if it isn't your Dr. Mont looking for revenge, who do you think it is?" Brad asked.

Wendy and Henry looked at him. Henry shrugged his shoulders, indicating he didn't know. Wendy shook her head, and told him, "Not a clue."

"And, you're sure, Wendy, that he didn't tell anyone?" Brad asked.

"He told me he would never say anything. I do know he's still good friends with the Masons. But I really don't think he would have said anything to them."

"I thought Donna's parents moved out of town."

"No. They have their house up for sale, but they are still living here in Kalispell," Wendy said.

"I've got to go. Jean's waiting for me," said Henry. "It was great seeing you, Brad. You, too, Wendy. But, as far as I can see, this little breakfast was a waste of time."

"Not really," said Brad. "At least, not for me. Good seeing you, too. My best to Jean."

"I've got to get going, too," said Wendy, as she watched Henry leave the restaurant. "Take care of yourself, Brad."

"You, too. And, make sure you watch your back."

Brad asked for another cup of coffee, sat back in

the booth, and thought about the conversation he'd just had with Wendy and Henry. He wondered if Henry was telling the truth. He couldn't imagine Henry pretending not to remember that night and never saying a word to anyone, especially his wife. Brad was sure he would have told his wife if he had one. Either Henry was lying or was an excellent actor. Detective Myers had told him that Henry had an airtight alibi and wasn't considered a suspect. He's strange now, Brad thought. Was he always such a weird character?

Wendy had certainly changed. She didn't remind Brad of the shy, cautious little girl he once knew. God, she is beautiful, he thought. I'd love one hour in the sack with her. I bet she could teach me a thing or two. He smiled, thinking about the flirting that had just taken place between the two of them. She may love that old doctor, but she's not above playing with us young guys. She had told the doctor about the fire. Right now, Brad decided, the doctor was the best suspect there was. He had told Myers that he had been with Wendy the night Brad's house was blown up. He might be Wendy's alibi for that night, but does the old doc have an alibi for the next morning, when Sarah was killed? Maybe, Brad thought, they're alibiing each other.

Brad glanced at his watch. He had a meeting with Detective Myers at 1:00. He decided to call and ask him if he could move it up a little. He was anxious to get back to Helena, and perhaps he could still leave today and get out ahead of the Labor Day traffic.

Twenty-one

Brad walked into the Kalispell Police Department thirty minutes after calling Detective Myers. The Desk Sergeant looked up, pointed Brad in the right direction when he asked about Myers, and went back to checking his email.

As Brad walked through the door, Myers stood and greeted him. "Have a seat," Myers said.

"Thanks for seeing me early. I'm anxious to get back home and meet with my insurance guy. Maybe we can get the ball rolling before the long weekend. I have to say, though, I'm not that anxious to see what's left of my home."

"I'll tell you right now, according to Detective West, it's bad. You know him, right?"

"West? Yea, I know him. He's a good cop. Well respected in Helena."

"You're right. I've known him for years. Anyway, he told me that there's not much left of your house."

"I've been thinking about that, Detective. I'm wondering if my house being blown up has anything to do with the murders."

"Really? What makes you say that?"

"If the same person, who killed my friends, was trying to kill me, why change his modus operandi?

Why not stab me and set me on fire, like the others? There are several people who don't like me in Helena. At least, they don't like the business I'm in. So, why blow up my house and not my bar?"

"Why bomb your house and not your business? I see where you're going with this, Brad, but at this point, I'm going to figure it's the same person or persons."

"Well, I think we should pursue both areas or at least keep an open mind. That note I got said that they hoped when I burned, I burned slow. Nothing slow about being blown up."

Myers was quiet, considering what Brad had said. "You know what? I'm going to call Detective West and tell him you're going to be back in town tonight. He and I are working together on these cases, so maybe he should check out your theory about the explosion. Why don't you make a list of everyone you know that would like to see your nudie bar closed down? Plus, anyone that might have a grudge against you for any other reason."

"That's gonna be one hell of a long list, Detective. It's gonna be mostly wives who can't control their men."

Myers laughed. "Well, you know Montana has a

lot of holy-rollers that don't like your type of business."

"Hell, nobody ever admits they like my business until they're putting dollar bills inside the dancers' g strings. Then, it's a different story."

"Have you remembered anything else that might be of use?"

"I might have a couple of things. I had breakfast with Wendy Berg and Henry Pullman this morning. It was kind of interesting."

"Do you think that was a good idea? After all, one of them might be trying to kill you," Myers said.

"I do think it was a good idea. You know why?"

Myers looked at him and grinned. "No, Brad, I don't know why. Why don't you tell me?"

"Because, Detective," Brad said, smiling, "Wendy told."

"Told what? Do you mean about the fire? She told someone? What about your pact?"

"Hey, I broke it when I told you. The pact is broken."

"Who did she tell? Wait – don't tell me. She told her boyfriend, Dr. Mont."

"You got it right the first time. Although, calling him her boyfriend kinda makes me want to puke. He's old."

"Watch it, kid. He's not that much older than me."

"But, boyfriend? I don't know. It kind of grosses me out."

"So, Dr. Mont knows why Peter died. I could see that he might want revenge."

"That's not all," Brad said.

"What?"

"Dr. Mont is good friends with Donna Mason's parents. There's a possibility he told them. That also gives them a motive."

"You're just an encyclopedia full of knowledge. I guess that breakfast was a good idea. Except, we've checked all the alibis and got nothing."

"Henry Pullman has been faking all these years. He remembers everything and has pretended he has selective amnesia, so he wouldn't have to talk about it," Brad said.

Myers sat back in his chair and stared at Brad. "Are you shitting me? He remembers everything?"

"Everything," Brad answered.

"Go on. What else should I know?"

"Wendy is one hot bitch."

Myers cracked up laughing and said, "That is something we already know, but thanks for the reminder."

"One other thought. It's probably nothing," said Brad. "Did you check out Dr. Mont's whereabouts on the morning Sarah was killed? Wendy says he was with her on Sunday when my house blew. But, what about the next day?"

"Son of a bitch. That's it," yelled Myers. "That's what has been gnawing at me for days. He alibied Wendy, but we never checked him out."

"Wendy told him in either May or June how Peter died. She can't remember which. But it wasn't long before the murders started." Brad moved forward in his chair and started to stand. "That's it for me. I've told you all I can remember. Unless you have more to talk about, I'd like to get going."

"I have to admit, I had second thoughts when you told me about having breakfast with Wendy and Henry. But that was a great idea, Brad. Maybe now I can get some answers. You've been a great help."

"Hey, I've lost some good friends. Especially Sarah. I loved her like a sister. If there is anything else I can do, let me know."

"I will. You can expect to hear from Detective West. Drive safe, Brad. Thanks again.

"No problem. Later, Detective."

Myers watched as Brad left the room. That's one hell of a sharp kid, he thought. He picked up the phone and called Detective West.

Twenty-two

Detective Myers' conversation, with Detective West, had moved on from discussing the information Brad had given him to what the coroner had found during Sarah's autopsy.

"Is it the same brand as the others?" Myers asked.

"The same. There's no doubt that we are dealing with the same person or persons."

"Where did you find it? I thought your guys did an area search where she was found," said Myers.

"It wasn't left at the scene, Morris. The coroner, Doc Martin, found it inside her when he did his autopsy."

"What else did he find? Was she alive when set on fire?"

"No. There wasn't smoke in her lungs. The Doc said she was definitely dead when put back in the car. The fire was mostly contained in the back seat, although she did have a few burns. There was more smoke than fire. Although, if that couple hadn't called it in, who knows what would have happened? The whole car might have gone up in flames."

"Do you know who the couple was who stopped and called the Highway Patrol?"

"Unfortunately, no. The patrolman never asked their names. Just thanked them and sent them on their way. He's been reprimanded, believe me."

"No plate number or description of the car?"

"He remembers they were driving an older model Toyota Camry. At least he thinks it was a Camry. Dark blue. That's not much to go on."

"No, but I can check to see if anyone here has a car like that. I doubt that will go anywhere, though. It probably was just a nice old couple doing the right thing," said Myers.

"Probably," West agreed. "You don't find many people doing that these days. The right thing, I mean."

"You'll check with Brad then? He should be back in Helena later today."

"I'll give him a call first thing in the morning. Do you know where he'll be staying?"

"He didn't say, but his guest house is still standing. He'll probably stay there or with a friend. We didn't discuss it," replied Myers.

"I'll let you know if I find out anything, Morris," said West.

"Back atcha. Take care," replied Myers.

What should have been a three-hour and

twenty-minute trip took Brad two and a half hours. He was back in Helena a few minutes after one. It took another twenty minutes to reach what had once been his home. He was sitting in his car, staring at the devastation. I could have been in there, he thought. I'd be dead. I wouldn't be sitting here. Or, anywhere.

He got out of the car, legs just a little shaky. He laughed to himself. Man, he thought, this is hitting me worse than I thought it would. He sat back down in the car, feet still on the ground. He scrolled through the numbers in his phone, found the one for his insurance agent, and called.

Sammy, his agent, said he would come over right away. Brad exited the car for the second time and walked closer to take a better look. His emotions were running wild. He wanted to cry over his loss, but, at the same time, he was happy to be alive.

He walked to the guest house and went inside. Four boxes were sitting in the middle of the living room. He reached for an envelope that was on top of one of the boxes and opened it.

"We packed up everything that was still intact and what we thought might be important to you. Love, your staff."

And, then, Brad totally lost it.

Dr. Mont was ready to blow. He had been sitting in an interrogation room for over thirty minutes. His phone had been confiscated, and the coffee that tasted like tar had gone cold. Try as he might to calm himself down, he knew his blood pressure was off the charts. He decided he'd had enough of this bullshit and decided to leave. If anyone tried to stop him, he was going to beat the crap out of them.

Just as he reached for the door handle, the door swung open and Detective Myers walked in. Mont moved back a little, then stopped and just stood there, blocking Myers' entrance.

"You need to move, Doctor," Myers said. "You're blocking my way."

"I'm leaving and it's you who is blocking my way, Myers. Move your sorry-ass body right now," Mont yelled. "I've had enough of your shit. This is harassment. I want my phone. Right now! You hear me, you piece of shit."

"Whoa, there, doc. What's got your undies in a bundle? You better settle down, before you have a heart attack."

"I'm done with this. I want my lawyer. I'm not saying anything until he gets here."

"Sit down. You're overreacting. I just want to ask you a couple of questions and then you can go."

"And, you can go to hell," Mont yelled.

"Sit. Down. Now," Myers said, so quietly Mont could barely hear him.

He glared at Myers, walked back to the chair, and sat. "Happy now?" he muttered.

"Doesn't make a whole lot of difference if I'm happy or not, does it? Can I freshen up your coffee? Perhaps, you would like a soft drink. Anything?"

Mont picked up his styrofoam coffee cup and shoved it at Myers. "This is not coffee. I don't know what the hell it is, but it definitely isn't coffee."

"Whatever," said Myers. "When did Wendy Berg tell you how and why your son died?"

Dr. Mont sat back in his chair and looked at Myers. "I don't know what you're talking about."

"And, I've had enough of your crap. When did she tell you?"

Mont sighed. "I think it was sometime the first week in June. Or, the end of May. No, definitely June. June 6th."

"What kind of a car do you drive?" Myers asked, totally changing the subject.

"What? What do you need to know that for?"

"Just answer me. What kind of cars do you have?"

"A 2015 Infinity."

"You just own the one car?" Myers asked.

"That's the only one I drive."

"That wasn't the question."

"I still have the car my wife used to drive. I never drive it, though. It's been in my garage for years."

"What kind?" Myers asked.

"It's a 2005 Corolla."

"What color?" asked Myers.

"Blue. It's a dark blue."

"Have you told anyone else about what happened the night your son died?"

"No," Mont replied.

"No one?"

"No one," Mont said, raising his voice. "Are you fucking deaf?"

"So, if I talk to the Masons, will they deny you told them about that night?"

Mont didn't say anything. He slowly started to push his chair back from the table. "I've answered enough of your questions, Myers. Either arrest me or let me leave."

"So will they?"

Dr. Mont shrugged. "How should I know what they will say?"

"Did you tell them, Doctor?"

"I might have mentioned something about it. I don't really remember."

"You don't remember if you told them? How can you not remember who you told? Did you tell so many people that you can't remember them all?"

"I might have mentioned it to a few people."

"Who'd you tell, Doctor? I want their names."

"Besides the Masons?" Mont asked.

"Yes, besides the Masons," Myers answered.

"I told the Lockharts. After Emma killed herself. I thought they should know what happened. Then, when Albert was murdered, I told his parents. That's all, though. That's all I told."

"Where were you on Monday, the 31st?"

"I was with patients. I was in town all day."

"Where were you the day before – on Sunday?" Myers asked.

"You know where I was. I was with Wendy. I already told you that."

"That's right, you did. You're her alibi. I know she was at work the next morning. Where were you Doctor, the next morning?"

"I suppose I did my rounds at the hospital and then saw patients, just like I do every day."

"Not that day. You didn't see patients that day, and you weren't at the hospital. So, exactly where were you?"

"I want my lawyer, Detective."

"Of course, you do."

Twenty-three

Detective Myers had enough information to obtain a search warrant for Dr. Mont's house. He wanted to see the car that supposedly had been sitting in Mont's garage for years. Mont had said it was a Corolla and the patrolman said he thought the car the couple was driving was a Camry. Both had said it was dark blue. Close enough, Myers decided.

Myers knew he could detain Mont for forty-eight hours without arresting him. So, while Mont was fuming back at the police station, Myers was opening Mont's garage door to take a look at the car. His men were in Mont's house already, searching for anything that might tie Mont to the murders.

Myers swore. No way had this car left Mont's garage earlier in the week. It was covered with years of dust, and it had two flat tires.

The search of the house came up empty. Myers went back to the station, knowing that he had to send Mont on his way.

An hour later, Myers was looking at a computer printout showing the description of the cars the suspects owned. He checked off all the cars that were 2014 or 2015 models or light-colored. That left four cars. The Freemans owned a 2010 black Toyota Rav4. Check. Henry Pullman's parents owned a 2012 black Ford Edge. Check. Donna Mason's parents owned a 2011 Blue Nissan Maxima. Myers straightened up in his chair. Okay, he thought. This might be something to check out. He glanced at the last unchecked car on the list and smiled. Wendy Berg owns a dark blue 2012 Toyota Camry.

"I'm sorry, Detective, but I can't help you. I traded that car in a couple of months ago," Wendy Berg said.

"For what?" Myers asked her.

"If you look out that window over there, you'll see a 2015 Avalon. Beautiful car. I absolutely love it."

"The paperwork for your old car is still in your name."

"Not my problem. I signed the title over to the dealer. It's not my fault if they are slow to transfer it."

"Did you buy that Avalon from a dealer here in town?" Myers asked.

"I sure did. Henry works there. I bought it from him."

"Henry Pullman?"

"He's worked there for years. Best salesman they

have, as far as I'm concerned. He gave me a great deal."

"Well, I'll let you get back to work. Thanks for your help."

Wendy smiled at him. "No problem. You can come visit me anytime." Slight hesitation showed on her face and then she asked, "Are you married, Detective?"

Myers grinned. "No ma'am, I most certainly am not. I enjoy the single life way too much to be tied down."

"Would you like to go out sometime? You know, for dinner or to a movie."

"How old are you, Wendy? Twenty-eight or twenty-nine? I think you're just a little young for me, don't you?"

"James didn't think I was too young for him. I'm sure he's a lot older than you."

"Are you two no longer a couple?"

"I broke it off with him. It's complicated, but let's just say it's for the best. So, are you interested? Or, are you involved with someone?"

Myers smiled. "It's certainly tempting, Wendy. There's no doubt you're probably the most beautiful woman in Kalispell. If I was . . . ."

"twenty years younger," she interrupted. "Or, if I was ten years older. God, I'm so sick of hearing that. What difference does age make? You're interesting and extremely good-looking. My god, look at your hair. I just want to run my fingers through it. I would like nothing better than to . . . "

"You know what, Wendy? It's not going to happen. I'm not interested."

"Of course, you are. Every man I meet wonders how to get into my pants. What makes you different?"

"I guess my pappy would just call it common sense. He taught me a long time ago to stay away from rattlesnakes or I'll get bit."

Wendy laughed. "Are you calling me a rattlesnake, Detective?"

"I'd say you're just as lethal."

"Think about it. Call me if you change your mind."

"Ma'am," Myers said as he turned and walked out of her office.

"And, don't call me ma'am. I'm not your damn mother," she yelled after him.

Myers figured Donna Mason's parents would be at work but decided to stop by their house anyway and check it out. Nothing suspicious had surfaced when they had been previously questioned. However, they owned a car that closely matched the description of the car the couple, who called the State Patrol, had been driving.

When Myers rang the bell, Mrs. Mason answered the door looking like she had just crawled out of bed.

"Sorry if I caught you at a bad time, Mrs. Mason," Myers said. "I was wondering if I could speak to you and your husband. I just have a couple of questions I need to ask you."

Barbara Mason stared at him. "Do I know you?" she asked.

"I believe we've met on a few occasions. I'm Detective Morris Myers with the Kalispell Police Department."

"I don't know you."

"Is your husband home, ma'am? Perhaps you can get him for me."

"My husband works. What? Do you think we're so rich we can sit around the house all day, doing nothing? Or, maybe fly off on some fancy vacation in the islands?"

"No. I don't think that. May I come in? This

won't take long."

"No, you may not come in. I don't let strangers into my house," she said and slammed the door in his face.

Myers stood on the porch, wondering what the hell had just happened. He had known Barbara Mason for almost twenty years and she didn't recognize him. He needed to talk to her husband, now.

Twenty-four

Cole Mason was standing behind the counter, waiting on a customer. He had worked at Finnegan's Discount Store for as long as Myers could remember. God, he looks old, thought Myers, as he waited for him to finish up the sale. Old and tired is being kind. He looks like he's ready to collapse.

The customer walked away and Cole Mason looked up and noticed Myers watching him. He gave Myers a weak smile. "What can I do for you, Myers? Are you here on business or do you need something?"

"Is there someplace where we can talk, Cole? I only need a few minutes of your time."

"Sure thing," Mason said and called over to his boss that he was taking a break. "Let's go to the break room and sit. I need to get off my feet for a few minutes, anyway."

Myers followed Mason into a room at the back of the store. He glanced around and noted that it was just like all the break rooms he had seen. There was a small table with a few chairs, a couple of lockers where the employees could put their stuff, a counter that held a coffee pot with all the fixings, and a refrigerator.

"Can I get you something?" Mason asked. "Juice, pop, water? I could make a pot of coffee, but it's a little late in the day for that. The boss frowns on us making coffee after three o'clock."

"I could use some water if it's no trouble," Myers said.

"Not at all." Mason took a bottle of water from the frig, handed it to Myers, and sat down at the table. "What can I do for you?"

"I was just at your house, Cole."

Cole took a deep breath and let it out. "Did you talk to Barbara?"

"I tried. She didn't know who I was. She looks terrible. And, so do you, by the way. What the hell is going on, Cole?"

"I haven't slept in ages. I mean a good night's sleep. She roams. All night, she roams around the house. She sleeps all day and then she's up most of the night. She blasts the TV or runs the vacuum cleaner. Then, she's gone, for hours at a time. She goes for walks in the middle of the night, for crying out loud. I go looking for her, hoping she hasn't been murdered or raped by some maniac roaming the streets."

"How long has this been going on?"

"The past few months."

"Since Dr. Mont told you how the fire started?"

Mason's head jerked up. "You know about that? How did you find out?"

"People talk, Cole. Have you taken Barbara to a doctor? It's obvious she needs some help," Myers said.

"She'll get over it."

"What if she doesn't? What if she hurts herself or gets hurt? You need to get her some help. And, you need some rest."

"I know. You're right. I've put it off too long. I'll do something about it."

"Good," replied Myers. "We're you in town on Monday and Tuesday?"

"In town and working. Your men already questioned me."

"What about Barbara? Can you account for her whereabouts?"

"Come on, Myers. You don't think Barbara drove all the way to Helena, blew up Brad's house, killed Sarah Compton, and then drove back home, do you?"

"Anything's possible."

"Well, she was here in town."

"You still have that Nissan?" Myers asked.

"Sure do."

"Is that your only car?"

"It is."

"Is that it, sitting outside there?"

"It is. I drive it to work every day."

"What does Barbara drive?"

"Barbara doesn't drive, Myers. She hasn't driven a car in years."

"Why not?"

"You probably wouldn't know this, or maybe remember it, but she had a bad car accident."

"I didn't know that. What happened?"

"Barbara was six months pregnant when a car sideswiped her and she hit a telephone pole. The driver of the other car was drunk. She was banged up pretty bad and she lost the baby."

"I'm sorry. How long ago did that happen? I don't remember it."

"It happened three days after we lost Donna. We buried the baby with Donna. We've spent the past sixteen years trying to get past this, and then that son of a bitch Mont tells us that story and brings it all up again. Why couldn't he have just kept his big mouth shut?"

"Believe me, I wish he had. He talked and that started all this mess. Someone is looking to get even."

"It's not us, Myers. I guarantee it. Donna's death was an accident. Those kids were just playing a game that went wrong. That driver that hit my wife – well, that's another story. But we've dealt with it for years. Now, this, with Barbara. It breaks my heart."

"I am so sorry. I really am. Let me know if there's anything I can do.

Cole Mason smiled at Myers. "I will, right after I figure out what the hell I can do. Thanks, anyway."

"Take care of yourself, Cole." Myers stood, shook Mason's hand, and left the building.

"I've concluded that the couple driving the dark blue car had nothing to do with this," Myers told West.

"You sure?" West asked.

"No. Unless they rented a car. We checked into that, too. Nothing came up."

"So, you have nothing?"

"Which is the same as what you've got," replied Myers.

"Not really," said West.

"You got something?"

"The fire investigator checking out the explosion at Brad's found something. He's still compiling the information, but he has submitted a preliminary report."

"What did he find?"

"A gas leak."

"What? It wasn't a bomb?" Myers said, raising his voice.

"Nope. One of the caterers was going to heat up something in the kitchen and turned the gas on but the burner never lit. She didn't notice it. Then, Brad read the card, called off the party, and told everyone to leave. She left with everyone else, forgetting about the stove. It took a while, but when an automatic timer turned off a light around two o'clock, there was a spark, and that's all she wrote. The gas had been leaking for hours, so it didn't take much. Brad had already packed up and got the hell out of Dodge, as they say."

"So, if Brad hadn't read that card, none of it would have happened. The caterer would have heated up whatever it was, turned off the burner, and the party would have continued, Brad would probably have gotten wasted and gone to bed, and the house would still be standing. The big question is, who wrote the note and laid it on the table for Brad to find," said Myers.

"Exactly. I can answer half of that question. We took handwriting samples from all his employees and the caterer's people working at the party. They all came up clean," said West.

"So, what do . . . "

"Hold on, Myers," West interrupted. "I'm not done yet. We know who put it there."

"You do?"

"Yep. A woman named Hillary Henson. She works for the catering company. We brought in all the employees, who worked the party that day, to get samples of their handwriting. We told them we had found fingerprints on the envelope and we were going to take their prints for comparison. She broke down and confessed."

"What connection does she have with all this?"

"None. A man approached her and asked her to slip the envelope in with the gifts. He offered her a fifty for her trouble. It seemed harmless enough to her, and it was easy money, so she did it."

"Description?"

"The guy is in his late forties or early fifties. Nice looking, kind of tall, brown eyes, and graying. I'm getting a picture line up together of all of your suspects."

"So, it was probably the father of one of the kids. Good work, Stan. That should narrow it down some."

"Let's just hope we get a hit."

Twenty-five

Brad Weiss was relieved when he found out that no one had tried to blow him up, yet his life had still been threatened. He decided to reside at the bar for a while, rather than use his guest house. The guest house was larger than the efficiency apartment on the upper level of the bar, but his house was on the outskirts of town and secluded. He figured he would be safer staying in town until his friends' murders were solved.

Detective West, from the Helena Police Department, had called him late Thursday night and informed him that the explosion had been an accident. He mentioned to Brad that they had no leads on the note, but were working on it and hoped that Hillary Henson would be able to identify the man from a picture lineup. He also told Brad to watch his back and suggested he try to avoid being alone if at all possible.

Brad was sitting at a table in his bar, phone in hand, drinking orange juice. He hesitated, wondering if making this call was a good idea. He had known Skunk since moving to Helena, and, although Skunk was probably the most unpleasant-smelling person he had ever met, he knew how to get things done. If you needed anything, Skunk was the guy to go to.

Brad felt sorry for the guy. Skunk had once told him that he showered at least three times a day, and practically lived on breath mints, but nothing helped. He had a condition called trimethylaminuria, better known as Fish Odor Syndrome. He could only hope that the intensity of the odor would diminish over time. Brad thought that it had diminished a little, as he found he could stand a little closer when meeting with Skunk these days. But, because of his condition, most of Skunk's business took place over the phone.

Brad finally decided Skunk was his best bet, punched in a phone number, and hit send.

Detective Morris Myers sat at his desk, took a sip of cold coffee, and put down his pen.

Emma's and Albert's murders were already over a month old and he had nothing. The killer could be anyone and everyone he questioned had an alibi. Forensics had come up with little to work with. Two scalpels, which anyone could have purchased, were about all he had. Hopefully, West's picture lineup might give them something.

Emma hadn't been burned, though, like Albert. He wondered if the killer had panicked before he had a chance to set her on fire. The park was a pretty open spot, but it had been late. There wouldn't have been many people around that time of night. Something had either scared him off or he decided to up his game and added burning the bodies when he killed Albert. The Autopsy Game had been Emma's idea. Did the killer know that and that's why she was the first to die? Albert was the one who cut Henry and he was the second. What was Sarah's sin that made her third on the list, Myers wondered.

He had little to go on and his suspect list was short. Short's good, he thought. He picked up the paper and read through it again. It's definitely not Wendy Berg or her parents, who reside in Idaho. Wendy was at work when Sarah was murdered and her parents were working on their farm. He smiled when he thought about Wendy's invitation. It was tempting. She wasn't just gorgeous, but she was extremely smart and interesting. Myers shook off his daydreaming and continued reading.

Albert Freeman's parents were in the clear, as were Emma Lockhart's and Sarah Compton's. In a sense, they were victims, also. They had to go on living knowing that their children had been murdered because they had played a dumb game sixteen years ago.

Myers was pretty sure that Brad Weiss and his parents had nothing to do with the murders. Donna Mason's mother belonged in a hospital and didn't drive and her father was at work when Sarah was killed.

That left Dr. James Mont and the Pullmans. Henry was at work when Sarah was killed. His parents, however, were on the shortlist. They had told him that Henry didn't remember anything about that night. Perhaps, they had also heard the story of what happened that night and wanted revenge. Wendy had told Dr. Mont. Who knows how many people he might have told and then those people told people and on and on? Plus, Mont didn't have an alibi at all.

Then, there are siblings, aunts, uncles, cousins, grandparents, and great-grandparents that could be looking to get even. And, how can I be sure that the same person killed all three of them, he wondered. Perhaps, it was someone living in Helena that took out Sarah and a totally different person who took out Emma and Albert.

"Fuck it!" he said, making the other officers in the room look up from their desks.

"Sorry," he said. "This case is driving me nuts. I'm out of here until Tuesday. You all have a good weekend."

Twenty-six

Skunk had come through for Brad. Not only was No Neck Washington one of the biggest guys that Brad had ever seen, but he was also probably the quickest. For two days now, except for bathroom visits, No Neck hadn't let Brad out of his sight. He would check the bathroom before Brad entered and stand guard outside the door until Brad finished his business.

If someone came too close to Brad or even looked slightly threatening, No Neck stepped in and steered the guy in a different direction. He checked out the apartment before Brad went upstairs to bed, and was waiting for him in the bar when Brad came down in the morning. Brad had never felt safer in his life.

Brad already had bouncers working for him. There were usually a few fights every night that his bouncers had to break up. Since No Neck had been on the premises, there hadn't been so much as a scuffle. Just No Neck's presence seemed to be enough to keep everyone in line. Brad was seriously considering hiring No Neck full-time after the killer was caught, although he doubted he could afford him. Right now, having No Neck guarding him was costing him a small fortune. The guy certainly didn't come cheap.

It was five o'clock, the Sunday before Labor Day,

and Brad was sitting at the bar, getting the banks ready for the night shift bartenders. No Neck was sitting at a table, having a cup of coffee. Although the strippers didn't start dancing until seven o'clock, there were already several men sitting at tables having drinks and talking. Music was playing in the background, and the place had a soft, comfortable feeling about it.

Brad expected a slow weekend, as many of his regulars would be out of town for a three or four-day vacation, or spending time at home with their families. Friday night had been a normal night for the Mounds and Mountains Strip Club, but Saturday's crowd surprised him. It was far more crowded than he expected, and many of the patrons were people he did not recognize. Now, just the fact that the bar was starting to fill up this early, on a Sunday before Labor Day, was extremely unusual.

He left the bar and walked over to a table where four men were enjoying a drink.

"Welcome to my place. I don't think I've seen you guys in here before. I'm Brad, the owner. Misty is your waitress, Just let her know if you need anything."

One of the men looked up and smiled. "We'll do that. Thanks."

"The entertainment won't start for a while. In the meantime, enjoy yourselves," Brad said.

"We didn't come here for the entertainment," one of the men replied. "We heard a giant was working here. We came to see him."

Brad laughed. "That would be No Neck, but he's not a giant. He's just a really big guy."

"I heard he's really tough. That's him over there, sitting at that table, isn't it?" the man asked. "I bet we could take him."

"First of all, this isn't a circus or a fight club and he's not the main attraction. If you're looking for trouble, I suggest you leave now," Brad said.

"You think you can make us?" one of the men asked.

"I know I can't, but I don't have to," Brad said, turned, and held up his hand. Immediately, two extremely large, muscular men appeared at the table.

"Trouble, Boss?" one of the bouncers asked.

"These gentlemen seem to have forgotten where the door is. Would you kindly point them in the right direction?"

"Hey, we're not doing anything wrong. You can't kick us . . . . "

Before the man could finish his sentence, one of

the bouncers grabbed him by the back of his shirt, pulled him out of his chair, and pushed him toward the door. As he started to grab for a second man, the man put up his arms and said, "I'm leaving. No need to get violent. We're all leaving, right guys?"

As the three men stood and started to walk out, the first guy, now standing at the bar's entrance, yelled, "Too bad you weren't in your fucking house when it blew. It would have been nice to see some garbage leave our town."

Brad watched as No Neck stood up and started to walk towards the man who had thrown out the insult at him. The man's mouth dropped open, he turned, and ran out the door. The other three men, who had stopped dead in their tracks when they saw No Neck stand up, suddenly found their feet and practically fell over each other racing for the door.

"Sons o'bitches, think I'm a sideshow. I'm no fucking sideshow," said No Neck.

"You certainly are not," said Brad. "You are a spectacular specimen of a man."

"Damn right," said No Neck, grinning. "That's me. Spectacular."

A gray-haired man, sitting at the far end of the

bar, frowned. He doubted very much that he would be getting close to Brad Weiss today. Maybe tomorrow, he thought. Or, a month from now. It makes no difference to me. I can wait. One thing's for sure, though. I'm looking at a dead man.

Twenty-seven

At ten o'clock on Tuesday morning, Detective West was sitting at Hillary Henson's kitchen table. She was studying the faces of eight men, who were part of the photo display that was lying on the table.

"What should I do if he's one of these men?" Hillary asked.

"I want you to be sure before you say anything. I'm going to record our conversation. If you pick out the man who paid you to put that card on Brad's table, then we will have another lineup. Except that one will be at the police station, and there will be six men standing in a lineup. They won't be able to see you, so you don't have to worry about that."

"What if he's not one of the men in these pictures?"

"Then we're done. I don't want you to say you recognize someone if you don't. The important thing is that we get an identification that will hold up in court. You need to be sure, Hillary."

She shook her head, indicating she understood what he was telling her. She smiled at West, said, "Here goes nothing," and continued to study the pictures.

West sipped his coffee and watched her. He was

intrigued by her concentration. She was examining each face as if her life depended on it. At one point she took her finger and traced the outline of one of the faces as if touching it would help her remember. West glanced down at his watch and realized that five minutes had passed.

Hillary glanced up at him and smiled. "You going somewhere, Detective?"

West laughed. "No, ma'am. I have to say, though, that I'm impressed. I've never seen a witness take more time or try to be more thorough."

"Well, I'm just trying to be sure. There's one face here that is close to the man who gave me the card. Except for the scar, I would say it's him."

"The scar? You never mentioned a scar."

"I forgot until now. The man that gave me the card had a scar on his chin. It was probably an inch or so long. When I looked at picture number three, I remembered the scar. If he had a scar and brown eyes, I would pick him. I'm sorry, Detective. It's none of these men."

"You're saying that the man who gave you the money looks like number three?"

"They're almost identical, except for the scar. And, this man has blue eyes, not brown like the man who gave me the card. I'm sorry."

"No. You may not have picked the guy, but you gave us his face."

"So, I did good?" Hillary asked.

"You did more than good. You did great. Thank you so much."

"You have a positive ID, then?" Myers asked.

"No. What I'm saying is that I almost have one. Hillary stopped short of identifying him from the picture because the man she saw had a scar. The man in the picture doesn't," West told him.

"So, he looks like the man in the picture, but isn't the man? Hillary is the woman who put the card on Brad's table?"

"Yes."

"And, she's reliable?"

"Very much so."

"So, we're possibly looking at a sibling. Someone who looks a lot like him, but with a scar," said Myers.

"Yes. And brown eyes, not blue. Did you know Mont is a triplet, Myers? One of his brothers, Robert, lives here in Helena and the other one, Richard, lives in Somers and works in Kalispell. There's another brother, but he's out east. We'll check him out, of course. He's a stockbroker in New York. He's nine years younger than his brothers. I doubt he's involved."

"Unless one of them has a scar, we can't assume any of them are involved."

"I'll bet my bottom dollar it's one of them," said West.

"Even if it is, we still don't have enough evidence to charge him with murder," replied Myers.

"It's a start."

"How's Brad doing? Watching his back?"

"Oh, he's definitely watching his back. He has, what can only be called a giant, guarding him."

"You're not talking about No Neck Washington, are you?" asked Myers, laughing.

"I certainly am. The baddest damn man in town. People are afraid to come within ten feet of Brad with No Neck standing there watching him."

"What's his story, anyway?" Myers asked.

"He was one of the largest babies born in Helena. Hell, maybe in the whole state or country. By his first birthday, he was almost three feet tall. He just kept growing until he topped out at seven and a half feet. He's huge, and most of it is muscle. He went to college for a few years and dropped out when he was offered a gig wrestling. He made good money, but his mama didn't like him doing it and made him quit. His mama, by the way, may be all of five feet, if that. He works for a moving company and does odd jobs, like what he's doing now working for Brad. There aren't a lot of people who need a personal guard around here, though. I heard he's charging Brad an arm and a leg for his services."

"So, you figure Brad's safe?"

"I figure he is, at least for now. No Neck is with him around the clock and the only way someone is gonna get past him is by either slipping No Neck a mickey or shooting him from at least twenty feet away."

"Okay, West, I'm going to start checking on his brother Richard. I'll let you know what I find out."

"Same here. Take care, Myers. Talk to you soon."

Myers found Richard Mont having lunch at Swenson's, a popular diner in downtown Kalispell. Swenson's had been there for close to seventy years, and except for an occasional paint job, it still looked the same as it had when Ole Swenson first opened it.

As Myers walked up to Mont's table, he immediately knew this was probably a dead end. The man had blue eyes and there definitely was no scar on his chin.

"Mr. Mont, I'm Detective Myers from the Kalispell Police Department. I'm sorry to bother you while you're having your lunch. I was wondering if I might join you for a couple of minutes?"

Richard Mont looked up at Myers, a questioning look on his face. "I'm sorta in a hurry, Detective. What do you want?"

"May I sit?"

"Sorry. Of course."

Myers pulled out a chair and sat down. "A person, who looks a lot like you, has been identified in a murder case being investigated in Helena. I was wondering if you could tell me where you were on August 30th."

"August 30th? What day was that?"

"It was a Sunday, sir. Do you remember where you were?"

Mont smiled at the detective. "I was in Vegas with my wife and a couple of friends. We flew out on Friday night and spent the weekend. Came back on Monday. It was a great trip, Detective. I won over $23,000.00. I'd say it was the best trip of my life."

"Your wife will verify your story, I assume?"

"Hell, yes. So will the couple we went with to Vegas and the manager of the casino. I don't know why anyone would say I did something in Helena. I wasn't anywhere near there. Your witness is way off base."

"May I have the name of the couple you were with?" Myers asked.

"Bill and Josie Smithers. You got a piece of paper on you? I'll give you their phone number."

Myers handed him a small notebook and watched as he wrote down the phone number. Mont handed it back to him and asked, "Is there anything else I can do for you, Detective?"

Myers smiled and stood up. "That's it for now. Again, I'm sorry I disturbed your meal."

"No problem," replied Mont.

Myers started to leave, took a few steps, and turned back to Mont. "By the way, I understand you have a brother, Robert, who lives in Helena."

Mont looked puzzled. "Yes, but . . . "

"And, you're a triplet, right?"

"Right, but I don't unders . . . "

"What color are his eyes?"

"What do you want to know that for?" Mont asked.

"What color are they?"

"They're brown, but I don't know why you need to know that."

"So, you're not identical triplets, then?" Myers asked.

"We look alike. The only real difference is that James and I have blue eyes and Robert's are brown."

"Thank you," said Myers. "Just one more thing."

Mont sighed. "What would that be, Detective?" he asked.

"Does Robert also have a scar on his chin?" Myers inquired.

Mont stared at Myers. He started biting his bottom lip and didn't answer.

"It's gonna be real easy to find out, Mont, so just tell me."

"Then go find out. I'm done talking to you," Mont replied.

Myers smiled and walked away.

Twenty-eight

Hillary Henson was standing in a small room staring at six men, who were on the other side of a large window. She was relaxed and focused. Detective West watched her and, again, marveled at her concentration.

The six men in the lineup were similar in height, weight, and looks. They all had dark brown hair and brown eyes. Three had identical scars on their chins, of which only one was real. Standing in position number five was Robert Mont.

"First, let me remind you that I am taping our conversation," said West.

"I remember. How did you manage to find three men with identical scars?" Hillary asked West.

West smiled. "We have our ways. Do you recognize anyone, Hillary?"

"I certainly do."

"Sooo?" West asked, dragging out the word.

"No question about it. It's number five," Hillary said.

"And, where do you know him from?"

"Number five is the man who paid me $50.00 to put a card on Mr. Weiss' patio table."

"Can you tell me where this table was located?"

"It was at his home, outside near the swimming pool," she replied.

"Do you remember when he did this?" asked West.

"Yes, sir, I do. It was on August 30th, of this year."

"Are you absolutely sure it is number five?"

"Absolutely," replied Hillary.

West turned to the man standing next to him. "Are you satisfied that this lineup was conducted properly and that no one coached Ms. Hanson?"

"I am," the man answered.

"Are you also satisfied that no one prejudiced her or interfered with her identification of the man wearing the number five in the lineup?

"I am."

"And, do you acknowledge that she identified this man as being the person who gave her the card to place on Mr. Weiss' table?"

"I do, Detective. This was a properly conducted lineup. Your witness identified my client, Robert Mont. I'm totally satisfied that this was handled in an extremely professional manner."

"Thank you," replied West. "I am now going to place Mr. Mont under arrest."

"What are the charges?" asked Mont's lawyer.

"For threatening Mr. Weiss' life. And, for the murder of Sarah Compton."

"Are you fucking nuts? You have nothing except a witness who says Mont gave her a note. You have nothing else. You try to arrest him for murder and I'll have your job."

"I want to talk to him," said West.

"Over my dead body. You've read him his rights. Now charge him with a misdemeanor and . . . "

"Oh, I'm going to charge him alright. And, it won't be a misdemeanor. I'm charging him with a felony. He wrote it down. It's a criminal threat. I'm gonna see his ass in jail."

"I'll have him out of here an hour after you charge him.

"We'll see what the judge has to say about that," West said. "And, even if he does get out, I'll have his ass right back in jail on a murder charge."

"Detective," said the lawyer. "Let me make it easy for you. Mr. Mont will admit he wrote the note and gave it to this young lady here. As far as Sarah Compton is concerned – well, let's just say he's got an airtight alibi for where he was when she was murdered."

"Really," said West. "Well, let's hear it."

"In due time," said the lawyer. "Everything in due time. Now, how about getting the paperwork rolling, so I can get Mont out of here?"

West turned to Hillary and said, "If you could stick around for a few more minutes, there are some papers I'd like you to sign."

"I'd be happy to Detective," she said.

It took more than an hour but by eight o'clock that night, Robert Mont was walking out of the Helena Police Station. He was free on a $50,000.00 bond. West was furious that the bond hadn't been set higher. Almost anyone could come up with $5,000.00 and Mont was no exception. It was now up to the D.A. to see to it that Mont was convicted on the charges.

At ten o'clock, Detective West called it a night and drove home. He ordered a pizza on his way, hoping it would be delivered right after he arrived home. It had been a long day, he had missed dinner, and he was starving.

Fifteen minutes later, his pizza arrived at the same time his phone rang. He answered the phone and asked the caller to hold, paid the pizza delivery person, and took the pizza from him. He walked to his kitchen, put the pizza on the counter, and put his phone to his ear.

"West here."

"Stan, this is Officer Lyle Blackstone. There's a problem at the Mounds and Mountains Strip Club. Thought you might like to know."

"What kind of a problem?"

"Looks like a 10-105."

"Who's the deceased?" West asked.

"Robert Mont," replied Officer Blackstone.

West looked around as he entered the strip club. Officer Blackstone had obviously segregated the patrons from the employees. He had also separated the dancers from the rest of the staff. Good work, West thought.

Then, he noticed Brad Weiss sitting at the bar talking to No Neck Washington. The coroner, Doc Martin, was kneeling over a body, which was on the floor. West motioned to Blackstone to join him.

Blackstone walked over to West. "What's the story, Lyle?" West asked.

"It seems that Mont came at Weiss with a knife. No Neck clotheslined him before he made it to Weiss. The hit was to his throat, and it seems that was just enough to break his neck. Doc figures he was dead before he hit the floor."

"One hit was all it took?" West asked.

"Just the one. Looks justified to me. No Neck was protecting his client as far as I can tell."

"Anyone over there see anything?" West asked, indicating the different groups of people on the other side of the room.

"A few. We're not done interviewing them yet. So far, they all say the same thing. Mont was sitting at the end of the bar, he suddenly yelled something at Weiss and charged. No Neck stepped in and that was that."

"God, he's huge," said West, looking over at No Neck. "I sure as hell wouldn't want to tangle with him."

"For sure," said Blackstone. "You'd have to be crazy to even try."

"Thanks," West said and walked over to Doc Martin.

"Whatcha got, Doc?"

"He's dead."

"You think?"

"His neck is broken. He probably died instantly."

"So, I heard. Self-defense?"

"Not for me to say. I just tag 'em and bag 'em.

But, from what I'm hearing, he came at Weiss with a knife."

"Thanks, Doc."

West started to approach Brad and No Neck but decided to stay back for a few minutes. Brad was hugging and telling No Neck, who was crying, that everything was going to be okay.

Brad looked over at West and indicated he would be with him in a few seconds. He handed No Neck a napkin and told him to blow his nose. He walked over to West.

"He saved my life, Detective. If it wasn't for him, I'd be dead right now."

"Maybe," said West.

"No maybes about it. I owe my life to him."

"Why's he crying?" West asked.

"He's afraid he's going to jail. He's never killed anyone before and it's a little traumatic. Plus, he's afraid of what his mama is going to say. Actually, he's probably more afraid of his mama than going to jail."

"Did you know the deceased?"

"Hell, no. I mean, I've seen him in here a lot lately. Almost every night. He comes in – sorry. He would come in and sit at the end of the bar, have a drink or two, and leave. He never really showed any interest in the dancers. I just thought he was some lonely guy. Then, tonight, as I walk towards him, he jumps off the stool and comes at me, yelling and waving a knife. No Neck stepped in and stopped him."

"So, you didn't recognize him? He's Dr. Mont's brother."

"This is Peter's uncle? I didn't know."

"They look a lot alike," said West.

"I haven't seen Peter's father in years. There's no way I would have put two and two together. But, why would he want to kill me?"

"Revenge for Peter, I guess. I figure he killed Sarah, but I may never be able to prove it. He wrote the note you got."

"This is the guy that threatened me? Are you sure?" Brad asked.

"Absolutely. He was positively identified in a lineup this afternoon. It was him."

"Why wasn't he in jail?"

"He was. We arrested him and when he was arraigned the judge set a low bail. He paid the bail and was back on the streets."

"Son of a bitch. So, he was just hanging around here looking for a chance to get me."

"Looks like it. I guess he figured he better try it

now or he may not get another chance," said West. "It doesn't fit the other killings though. Using a knife and it doesn't look like he planned to set you on fire."

"It wasn't a knife, Detective."

"I thought he came at you with a knife," replied West.

"It was a scalpel. Just like what killed my friends," said Brad. "Your policeman, the one standing over there, put it in an evidence bag."

"That's Officer Blackstone."

"Right. I forgot his name," said Brad.

"What did he yell?" asked West.

"I'm not sure. Maybe someone else heard what he said and can answer that for you."

"I hope so. Thanks, Brad. I want you to come down to the station in the morning and give an official statement," West said.

"I will. Is around ten good for you?"

"Call first just to be sure I'm in the office."

"Detective, could you go talk to No Neck? I can't stand to see him crying. Perhaps, you could tell him he isn't going to spend the rest of his life in jail."

"A big softie in a big body. I'll talk to him."

Twenty-nine

"We have enough to close the case on Sarah Compton, but I don't think it's going to help you much with the Lockhart and Freeman cases," West told Myers.

"Have you completed your search?" Myers asked.

"Just about. We found a knife that Doc Martin says is most likely the murder weapon. It's the right size and shape. It matches most of Sarah's stab wounds. Some of the lesser cuts were done with a scalpel. They're not as deep as the others. It looks like he sliced her open and then stuck the scalpel inside her when he was finished. I've seen rage, Myers, but this went way beyond angry."

"So, there's little doubt it was him. How did he manage to get her to pull over and then drive her car into that secluded area?"

"The damage on her car indicates that she was hit from behind. She probably pulled over and stopped. He could have had a gun. We don't know and we didn't find one. But, somehow, he managed to subdue her and then drove her and the car out of sight, where he killed her. It would make more sense, though, if there was more than one person. That way both cars would have been secluded and no one would remember seeing an empty car parked on the side of the highway."

"So, do you still think he was working with someone else?"

"It's possible. I figure it might be one of his brothers. Most likely the doctor. We found several texts on Robert's phone and emails on his computer between the two of them. The emails were about leaving the note for Brad, so we know that James was aware of what Robert was doing. We also found a box of scalpels in his house. A couple of them were missing."

"Do you know where he got them?" Myers inquired.

"We went through his Amazon account and found that he purchased them there. He also bought rubber gloves. We're still tracking down where he got the knife."

"That could be any hunting supply store," said Myers. "You know that James Mont hasn't got an alibi for the morning that Sarah was murdered. I wouldn't be surprised if the two of them killed her."

"Well, Myers, unless you can get him to confess to it, we'll never know. We have enough to know that

James was aware of what Robert was doing, but not enough for you to arrest him."

"Would you send me copies of those emails," Myers asked.

"As soon as we hang up," West replied.

"Have you notified Mont's family yet?"

"No. As far as everyone is concerned the body still hasn't been identified. The story we told the press is that some drunk went crazy in Brad's bar and attacked him. An unnamed gentleman helped to subdue him and the attacker suffered a heart attack. That's what today's papers are saying. Of course, anyone who lives around here and was in that bar knows who No Neck is. I'm sure that, by now, a lot of people know who the unnamed gentleman is.

"Does Mont have relatives in Helena? Wasn't he married?"

"Divorced. Never had any kids. I'm sure someone is going to miss him before too long, but I figure we have a day or more to go through his belongings before the word gets out."

"That also gives me a little time. I'm hauling in the good doctor's ass. He's going to get the questioning of his life."

"He'll lawyer up," stated West.

"Probably. But I figure if I let him know his brother is lying in a morgue and that you found his fingerprints on the scalpel, which was found inside Sarah, I might get lucky."

"Which we didn't. Can you get a search warrant?"

"I'm already on it. We need to check out James' computer and phone before he erases everything and makes our tech guy's job all the harder."

"Hopefully, this will put an end to the killings. I figure Brad is safe and I doubt anyone is going to go after Wendy Lockhart or Henry Pullman now," said West.

"Let's hope," replied Myers.

"I am, without a doubt, suing you, the Police Department, and the City of Kalispell for harassment. I am a doctor and I expect to be treated with respect."

"You are being treated with respect, Doctor."

"Coming into my office and slapping handcuffs on me, in front of my patients, is not showing respect."

"Were you read your rights?" Myers asked Dr. Mont.

"Yes, in front of my staff. I've never been so embarrassed."

"That's a shame. You are under arrest, Doctor. Do you understand that?"

"For what? I've done absolutely nothing wrong. I want my phone call," yelled Mont.

"You will get your phone call and, when you do, you can tell your lawyer that you have been arrested for threatening Brad Weiss' life."

"I did no such thing," yelled the doctor.

Myers reached over to switch on a tape recorder. Mont has asked for a phone call but he hasn't asked for his attorney. I wonder how long before he realizes his mistake, Myers thought to himself.

"Doctor, with your permission I will be recording our conversation."

"Whatever," said Dr. Mont.

"And, we are now recording," said Myers. "It is Thursday, September 10, 2015. I am Detective Morris Myers. Officer Kyle Henry is . . . "

"It's Detective Henry – not Officer," Detective Henry interrupted.

"Sorry, Kyle. To continue, Detective Kyle Henry is also present. I am interrogating Dr. James Mont. He has been made aware that this conversation is being recorded and has agreed to the same. Doctor, you have been arrested for threatening Brad Weiss' life and as a coconspirator in Sarah Compton's murder. We have evidence that you were aware that your brother, Robert Mont, planned to murder her and you did nothing to warn her. We believe that you took part in her murder and that you and your brother mutilated her body after you killed her. We also believe that you then assisted your brother in an attempt to burn her body, along with any trace evidence that might have been left behind."

Dr. Mont's face paled as he listened to Myers. "You think that Robert killed Sarah Compton? Have you gone completely crazy?"

Detective Myers didn't say anything. He simply opened the folder in front of him and pulled out several sheets of paper and laid them in front of Dr. Mont.

"Do you recognize these emails, Doctor," Myers asked and watched Mont's face turn from pale to bright red as he looked at them.

"Where the hell did you get these?" he screamed. "These are private."

"So, you admit you wrote some of these?" Myers asked.

Mont went silent. He looked confused as he stared at Myers. He hasn't quite put it together, Myers thought. Myers watched as Mont finally realized what was happening.

"If you think my brother murdered Sarah Compton – well, I know absolutely nothing about that."

"Let's start again. In front of you are emails that were written by you and your brother, Robert. They state that you are well aware that Robert threatened Brad Weiss. You were not only aware, but you encouraged him and helped him compose the note. What do you have to say about this, Doctor?"

Dr. Mont didn't respond.

"We also believe that you helped Robert murder Sarah Compton on August 31st of this year."

"I was nowhere near Helena that day. I was in my office."

"No, Doctor, you weren't. In front of you is an email indicating that you knew Robert was stalking Brad Weiss and intended to 'gut him like a pig', as he put it."

"Robert has problems. I didn't take him seriously. He was just blowing off steam. When we found out what had happened to Peter, it was like living that horrible night all over again. We were all upset. Yes, we talked about someone paying for his death, but it was just talk," Mont said.

"So, when you sent him back an email saying, 'go for it, the fucker deserves it' you weren't encouraging him?"

"Of course not," replied Mont.

"Do you know that your brother was arrested yesterday and was out on bond?"

"What? Of course not."

"So, if we check your phone, we won't find a call that took place last night between you and your brother?"

"Alright. Yes, I knew. He called me around eight o'clock and told me what had happened."

"Did he also tell you he was going to kill Brad?"

"No. I would have done something to stop him," said Mont.

"The Helena police found a text on his phone, to you, that was written last night right around ten o'clock."

"So? We text a lot. We're a very close family."

Myers smiled. "I believe you. His text was short. Only four words."

Dr. Mont didn't say anything.

"You remember what they were, Doctor?"

Mont stared at him.

"They were 'it's now or never,'" Myers said. "And,

just to refresh your memory, Doctor, you replied, 'go for it'. Seems like that might be your favorite phrase. Go for it. Remember that, Dr. Mont?"

Mont remained quiet.

"Why don't you start at the beginning and tell us the whole story? That way we will have the facts correct and will know exactly what to charge you with. With what we have right now, you may be spending the rest of your sorry life in prison. Talk and the judge may go easy on you for cooperating with us."

"I have nothing to say. I want my phone call now."

"Brad Weiss is still alive, Doctor. Your brother messed up."

"Why wouldn't he be alive? I have no idea what you're talking about," Mont said.

"Your brother texted you a few minutes before he tried to kill Weiss. You texted him back, saying he should 'go for it'.

"I never meant it. I didn't want him to kill Brad or anybody."

"Really? I'm sorry to inform you, Doctor, that your brother Robert died a few minutes after ten o'clock last night."

Dr. James Mont's head jerked up, and he stared

at Myers. His face turned white and he fell back in his chair.

"No," he said, so quiet you could hardly hear him.

"Yes," said Myers. "But he went for it, just like you told him to. He tried to kill Brad Weiss. In fact, he died trying."

Thirty

It was 6:46 a.m. in Kalispell, Montana. Detective Myers looked at his watch and stood. "It's time, guys," he said to his fellow officers. The seven other men in the room stood and turned to face the flag. They bowed their heads and were silent. It was 8:46 a.m. in New York City, and fourteen years after the terrorist attacks that killed nearly 3,000 people on September 11, 2001.

A minute later, Myers raised his head and said a silent amen. A number of the officers repeated his amen aloud and went back to work. Myers walked over to the coffee machine and poured his second cup of coffee of the morning. He had come in early, after finding it almost impossible to sleep the night before.

Dr. James Mont had spent the night in jail. Myers doubted Mont would be getting out on bond. He hoped that the judge would set the bail so high that Mont wouldn't be able to come up with the cash. Better yet, he hoped that Mont would be held without bond, although Myers figured that was probably not going to happen. If Mont was arraigned today, he would be home before the day was over.

It seemed logical that Robert and James Mont worked together and committed all the murders. There was no doubt that Robert killed Sarah and went after

Brad. Myers didn't doubt that James had killed Emma and Albert. He just didn't have enough evidence to prove it. Perhaps the CSI Unit, when they continued their search today of the doctor's, house, car, and office, would find something.

Myers spent the rest of the morning reading and re-reading the reports of Emma's and Albert's murders. Some, but not all, of the prints that had been found in Albert Freeman's car, had been identified. Kitty, the mother of Albert's young son, had been eliminated, as had his parents. Myers decided he wanted the prints from every close relative and friend of Donna Mason, Henry Pullman, and Peter Mont. Rather than obtain warrants, he decided to start by asking people to voluntarily give him their prints. Then, if necessary, he would obtain warrants for those who refused.

He had checked Dr. Mont's prints this morning and they had not been a match to any of the unidentified prints from Albert's car. Myers made up a list of individuals he wanted to get prints from and sent a couple of patrolmen out to obtain them. The list, among others, included Cole and Barbara Mason, John and Marianne Pullman, Wendy Berg, and her brother, Ted. If none of these panned out, he would expand the list. Hell, he thought, I'll print every damn person in Kalispell if I have to. But, one way or the other, I'm finding out who these prints belong to.

Dr. Mont walked out of the courthouse and got into the front seat of a car that was parked in front of the building. "Thanks for picking me up," he told the driver.

"No problem. How did it go?"

"Okay, I guess. I had to surrender my passport and they upped the bond to $200,000.00."

"You managed to come up with the 10% fast enough. You always keep that much cash on hand?"

"Gladys went to the bank this morning and withdrew $50,000.00 from my account. I was hoping that the bond would be under $500,000.00. I certainly didn't think the judge would go as low as he did," said Mont.

"I don't even know why that asshole, Myers, arrested you. They don't have anything on you."

"Actually, they do," said Mont. "They have emails and some texts that show I knew about Robert's plans and that I encouraged him."

"But they only mention the note, right?"

Mont didn't say anything for a few seconds.

"Right, James?" she repeated.

"Not exactly," Mont replied. "There are emails where he talks about killing Weiss. And, a few where I tell him to go for it."

"What the fuck is wrong with you?"

"I'm sorry, Marianne. Robert was wavering. I needed to convince him to go through with it."

"What's the next fucking thing I'm gonna hear? That you confessed to killing that fucking Freeman kid?"

"Just remember, you helped. Plus, you killed Emma Lockhart. If I go down, so do you. Besides, why would I confess? I have no great wish to spend the rest of my life in jail."

"Because you're a fucking idiot. You don't know when to keep your fucking mouth shut. And, you know I didn't kill that Lockhart bitch."

"Settle down, Marianne. I haven't told anybody anything. Even so, I'll still probably go to jail and lose my practice. And, quit the swearing, will you? It doesn't become you."

"Don't you fucking tell me what to do. I'll swear if I want to. And, you know I didn't kill her. She committed suicide."

"You called her, you met with her, talked her into it, and you handed her the scalpel. Basically, you murdered her."

"Where do you want me to drop you off?"

"At my house, please. I need to shower and get rid of the stink of that jail."

"What do you think, James? Are we safe?"

"As long as we keep our mouths shut and don't admit to anything, we should be okay," Mont replied.

"I'm scared."

"Just keep your mouth shut. Understand?"

Marianne Pullman gave him a nasty smile. "I, for sure, do fucking understand."

Detective Myers ran the plate number of the car that picked up Dr. Mont outside the courthouse. The car belonged to John Pullman. Myers figured the woman driving was John's wife, Marianne.

He followed them, staying a good distance behind until the car pulled over and stopped in front of Mont's house. He watched Mont get out of the passenger side of the car, slam the door shut, and walk towards the backyard. The woman pulled away from the curb and drove off. Myers followed her.

He picked up the two-way radio and contacted

his office, asking to speak to Detective Kyle Henry.

"Hey, Morris," answered Henry. "What do you need?"

"Did you get any hits off the fingerprints?"

"Not all of them are in yet."

"Did you get Marianne Pullman's prints yet?"

"Let me see. Doesn't look like it. We still need hers and, Ted Berg, Wendy's brother."

"I'm following Marianne Pullman right now. It looks like she's on her way home. I'm going to see if I can get her to agree to be fingerprinted."

"Why are you following her?" Henry asked.

"I saw her pick Mont up from the courthouse. I wanted to see where she was taking him," Myers said.

"Are you kidding me? I didn't know those two were close."

"Me either."

"Where'd she take him?" Henry asked.

"She dropped him off at his house. Okay, she's pulling into her driveway. I'll give her a minute before I go in. Thanks, Kyle."

Thirty-one

Marianne Pullman stopped and glanced in the mirror, which hung in the entryway of her home. She smiled at her reflection and said, "You still got it, kid."

She was almost fifty years old but people guessed her age as between thirty and thirty-five. The fact that she had some work done a few years ago helped, but she still considered herself a natural beauty. It wasn't unusual for younger men to hit on her. And, it wasn't unusual for her to respond to their advances and enjoy a quickie at the local Hotel Eight or the back seat of someone's car. She was a regular at The Lonely Steer Bar and could be found there two or three nights a week. The people, who still associated with her, considered her an alcoholic. Her husband, John, had given up trying to help her years ago. The fact that they stayed married confused their family and friends.

Myers gave Marianne a good five minutes before he exited his car and knocked on her front door. No answer. He knocked again, then noticed the doorbell and pushed the button. Still no answer. He was about to start pounding on the door, when it swung open and he saw Marianne, holding the front of a thin robe, in an attempt to keep it closed.

"Detective," she practically purred. "What can I do for you?"

"I was wondering if I could talk to you for a few minutes," Myers replied.

"I'm sorry, but I was just about to get into the shower. Perhaps, we can do this at a later time?"

"I'd like to do it now," Myers replied. "Perhaps you could throw on some slacks and a top."

"Perhaps I don't and we talk anyway. I'm sure you've seen women in robes before and I really don't feel like getting dressed again. You said all you need is a few minutes, so come on in," she said and held the door open so Myers could enter.

Marianne took a seat on the couch and Myers sat down on a matching chair, across the room from her. Marianne smiled at him. "I'd offer you a drink, but I really am in a hurry. What did you want to ask me, Detective? Or, perhaps I can call you Morris. Would that be okay?"

"I prefer Detective Myers, if you don't mind."

"You look nervous, Detective Myers. Do I make you just a little nervous?"

"No ma'am, you don't."

"You're not married, are you Detective Myers?"

she asked.

Ignoring her question, Myers said, "Could you tell me where you were on July 13th between 10:00 p.m. and 3:00 a.m. the following morning? Also, can you account for your whereabouts on July 27th, between 10:00 pm and 2:00 am?"

Marianne looked at him, with a confused look on her face. "Detective Myers, today is Friday, September 11th. Do you actually think I remember where I was on those nights?" She moved slightly, allowing the robe to fall far enough away from her leg, so her thigh was exposed.

"I was hoping you could," said Myers, concentrating on looking at her face.

"Those are the nights that Emma Lockhart and Albert Freeman died, aren't they?"

"Yes, ma'am," replied Myers.

"Well, the best I can do is check my calendar and see what I might have had going on. Right now, Detective Myers, I have no idea."

Myers watched as the robe slid to the side of her thigh. "You might want to cover yourself," he said.

"Or," she said softly, "you might want me to take it completely off. We could go upstairs if you want. I've got nothing else to do and you are one fine-looking detective."

"No. I have one more question to ask before I leave," Myers said.

"You sure you're not interested? You sure you wouldn't like to fuck me?"

"Are you drunk?" Myers asked.

"I might have had a drink or two, but I'm certainly not drunk."

"I'd like to take your fingerprints before I leave."

"I'll let you take my fingerprints if you fuck me," she said.

"That's a no," Myers commented.

"I think it has to be a no," Marianne said, laughing.

"Don't leave town, Mrs. Pullman. I'll be back with a warrant for those prints."

"Oh, good. You're coming back. Maybe, by then, you will have learned how to take your big boy pants off all by yourself."

Myers stood up and walked towards the door. He turned and looked at her, "I highly suggest you get some help," he said and walked out of her house.

"And, I suggest you go fuck yourself," she yelled, as he shut her front door.

Myers sat in his car, collecting himself. He wasn't a rookie and he knew that this kind of stuff went down all the time. It had been a while, though, since he had dealt with a nut like Marianne Pullman. He took a deep breath, started his car, and drove off.

"I must remember to bring someone with me when I serve that warrant," he said out loud.

The minute Myers got back to the police station, he started filling out the paperwork that was required for a judge to issue a warrant. As soon as he had the signed warrant, he planned on grabbing Detective Henry to go with him to the Pullman house. He did not look forward to that visit, figuring Marianne would make another scene.

While he waited for the warrant, Myers decided that he would take a drive over to The Lonely Steer Bar. The police had interviewed some of the employees and Albert's friends after Albert had been killed. They had all told the police that Albert was fine when he left the bar. Myers hoped the owner of the bar still had the video from the security camera from that night. He needed to take a look.

"Two more weeks and you'd have been out of

luck," the manager of The Lonely Steer Bar told Myers. "We save everything to the cloud and keep three months of videos at a time. We're charged a monthly fee and we've found that three months are the maximum number of videos we can save before the fee goes to the next level. So, we delete the oldest video every day. It's based on gigs, as I understand it. Anyway, we should be able to get you what you want."

"I want the night of July 27th. That's the night Albert Freeman was murdered. Wait, it's Sunday, the 26th. He was killed early Monday morning," said Myers.

"I'll download it to a flash drive. That way you can take a copy with you," the manager told Myers.

"Thanks. Will this take long?"

"Just a few minutes. Why don't you go get a cup of coffee from the bar?"

"I'd like to see how you do this. I've been thinking about saving the files on my computer to the cloud. Just wasn't sure if it's safe."

"Oh, it's safe all right. Your computer may crash, but your files will always be up there in the cloud."

Thirty-two

Myers spent a few hours Saturday morning reviewing the security video that the manager of the bar had given him. It showed Albert arriving at the bar, having a few drinks with his friends, and leaving at exactly 12:17 a.m. Nothing seemed out of the ordinary, and verified what the bartender and Albert's friends had told him.

When Myers watched the video the third time, he concentrated on the customers who were not part of Albert's group. He noticed something interesting in the upper right section of the video and hit the pause button. He backed it up a little, hit pause again, and zoomed in. "Son of a bitch," he exclaimed aloud, causing a few cops in the room to look up from their desks.

"You find something, Myers?" one of the cops asked.

"I may have. I just may have," Myers replied. He forwarded the video and then paused it when he noticed a man exiting a booth and walking out the front door. The timestamp said 12:05 a.m. He wrote down the time in his notebook and continued watching. At 12:10 a.m., the video showed that Albert pushed back his chair, rose, shook a few hands, and said goodnight to his friends. Myers paused the video again and made note of this. He hit the play button and watched as a woman slipped out of the same booth that the first man had occupied. At exactly 12:17 a.m., Albert walked out of the bar, directly behind the woman.

"Gotcha," Myers exclaimed.

The warrant for Marianne Pullman's fingerprints was modified to include her house and car. It was signed by the judge at 8:00 the following Monday. Detective Myers asked Officer Jane Widdell to accompany him and Detective Henry to the Pullman home, figuring that having a female officer present was a good idea. There was no telling what condition Mrs. Pullman would be in when they arrived and, if she was not properly clothed, Office Widdell was better equipped to handle the situation.

Marianne Pullman answered the door looking a great deal different than she had on Friday. Her hair was a mess, she was makeup-free, and she was wearing an old pair of jeans and a tee shirt. She was not wearing a bra under the shirt.

When Detective Myers asked if her husband was at home, Marianne laughed.

"You think he's here? He's never here," she said, angrily. "He leaves every Sunday afternoon and comes back home on Saturday morning. I doubt he would even do that if he didn't need clean clothes. I used to do his wash, but quit doing that when his clothes started to smell like some slut's perfume."

"Just what is his job?" Myers asked.

"He works for Montana Power and Light. Their home office is in Butte. I'll give you their number if you want it."

"Does he have a home there?"

"He rents a room at some boarding house. At least, that's what he tells me. I've never been there," she replied.

"Was he out of town when Emma Lockhart and Albert Freeman were murdered?" Myers asked.

"He's always out of town, Detective. He hasn't spent a full week with me in over two years. Now, if you don't mind, I'd like you to leave. I'm busy."

"I have a warrant that allows me to search your home and car. I'm also going to take your prints."

"You seriously think I'm going to let you touch me? You had your chance, you fairy."

"We can do it here or I can take you downtown. It's your choice."

"We can do it here or I can take you downtown," Marianne mimicked. "It's your choice – blah, blah, blah. Well, my choice is not to have my prints taken, and you sure as hell aren't going to search my house. Now, take your sorry-ass comic book cops and get the hell out of my house."

It took both Detective Myers and Detective Henry to get Marianne Pullman into the squad car. She screamed, kicked, hit Detective Henry, and tried to bite Detective Myers. They finally got the cuffs on her and deposited her, none too gently, into the back seat.

"You think you're so tough, don't you?" she yelled.

Myers laughed. "You're the tough one. I've arrested men who were easier to take down than you."

"This isn't funny," Marianne said and started crying. "I didn't do anything to have you treat me like this."

"You shouldn't have resisted us. Now you'll be arrested for obstruction and for striking an officer of the law. Just remember, it was your choice."

"You're lying," Marianne Pullman said. She had been left alone, sitting in a windowless room for over an hour. She was angry and she was ready to rumble. "There's no way my prints were in that car, Detective, and you know it. You're just saying that to upset me."

"Your prints are a perfect match. That, along with the other evidence we have, is all we need. Officer Widdell, will you please read Mrs. Pullman her rights?"

Officer Widdell gave Myers a big smile. "It's my pleasure, Sir."

"I'll be back in a minute," Myers said and left the room.

"Arrest me for what?" Marianne yelled as Myers left the room. She turned to Officer Widdell and asked, "How can you work with that man?"

"You got her?" Detective Henry asked when Myers stepped out of the interrogation room.

"I figure I do. Now I just need to get her to confess and bring down Mont with her."

"Has she lawyered up?"

"Not yet. I've got to hit now, while she's still hungover. I figure she could use a nice strong cup of coffee."

"Are you trying to sober her up?" Henry asked.

"It's decaf. I don't think that will hurt."

"It sure won't help – her, I mean," said Henry,

smiling.

Myers waited fifteen minutes before he went back into the room to talk to Marianne. She was sitting in the same chair, face down with her head resting on her arms, which were now cuffed. He placed a cup of coffee in front of her.

"It's freshly brewed, Marianne."

Marianne raised her head and stared at him.

"That lady cop cuffed me. Is this really necessary?"

"It is. You're under arrest. You'll be required to wear those bracelets, except for when you're in your cell, for the rest of your life. That is, if you're lucky, and don't get the death sentence."

"I didn't do anything wrong."

"Marianne, your prints were found in Albert Freeman's car. You were seen leaving The Lonely Steer Bar just seconds before him and right after Dr. Mont. We know that you and Mont killed him."

"I did no such thing. My prints were in his car because we had sex in his car."

"Did you have sex in the front seat or the back seat?"

"Both."

"Are you saying you had sex twice the same night, or you had sex on two different occasions?"

"On two different occasions."

"I didn't know you were a couple."

"We aren't. We just hook up once in a while. I get lonely and he filled a need."

"So, you admit that you hooked up with him the night he was killed?"

"Yes. No. I mean no. Not that night. I saw him at the bar, but I didn't talk to him."

"Who were you with that night?" Myers asked.

"No one. I was alone."

"I don't think so. We have you on video sitting in a booth with a man."

"You do?" Marianne said, hesitantly.

"We do."

"I think you're wrong. I was alone."

"Who was the man you were with, Marianne?"

"You know who it was, don't you?" she asked.

"We do, but I want to hear you tell me."

"James."

"James, who?"

"Dr. James Mont. Now, are you satisfied, you bastard?"

"Stay nice, Marianne."

"Fuck you."

"What did you and Dr. Mont do after you left the bar?"

"We went home."

"No, you didn't. You hooked up with Albert outside the bar, didn't you?"

"No."

"Yes, you did. And, while you distracted Albert, Mont hid in the back of his car, didn't he?"

"No, that's not what happened. You're so wrong."

"No, I'm not. And, then, Albert drove to his house and you followed him in your car. But, before he got out of the car, Mont hit him in the head with a hammer, didn't he?"

The door to the room opened and a cop motioned for Myers to join him.

"Not now, Pete," Myers said, aggravated at the interruption.

"You're gonna want to see this, Detective," Officer Peter Johnson said.

"Excuse me," Myers said. "I'll be right back."

"What the hell, Pete? You know better than to interrupt me in the middle of an interrogation. This better be good."

"Oh, it's good. We found one of Mrs. Pullman's blouses in the back of her closet. It's got blood on it. The same type of blood as Albert Freeman's. Doc Martin is checking it right now to see if it's a match."

"Are you kidding me? I know she's not the brightest person in the world, but any idiot would know enough to get rid of that kind of evidence. If it matches Freeman's blood, we got her for sure. I think I'm close to getting her to talk. She's a mess. I just need to get it done before she smartens up and lawyers up."

"We're still going through the house. The car was clean."

"It'll be great if you find something else. You got her phone and computer?

"Sure do. They're being looked at right now," said Officer Johnson.

"What color is the blouse? Is there a design to it?"

"It's pale gold. No, I guess it's yellow. It's got flowers on it. Daisies, I think they're called."

Myers smiled a huge smile. "That's what she was wearing on the video. It's going to be Freeman's blood on it, for sure. We got her, Pete."

Thirty-three

"Sorry for the interruption," Myers said, as he walked back into the interrogation room. "I just got some good news."

"Bully for you," Marianne said, sarcastically.

Myers sat down across from Marianne and smiled. He looked over at a small light on the wall to be sure they were being recorded. The light showed green. He was good to go.

"What's so damn funny?" she asked.

"I'm just so happy about what's going to happen," he replied.

"What's going to happen?"

"You are going to tell me all about how you and Dr. Mont killed Emma Lockhart and Albert Freeman. I'm recording this, by the way. You're going to start at the beginning, Marianne, and tell me the whole story. Most of all, I want to know why you killed two innocent people. I want to know the reason."

"Innocent?" she screamed. "They weren't innocent."

"Are you saying you killed them?"

"Of course not. I didn't kill them."

"Here's what's going to happen. We are going to arrest you for . . . "

"You already arrested me," she interrupted. "You can't do it again."

"But, we can. This time for murder. We have your blouse with Freeman's blood on it. We have a video of you and Mont in The Lonely Steer Bar, while Albert was there. We have you leaving the bar at the same time as Albert. We have your fingerprints in his car, which you left while helping Mont drag Albert's body out of the car and to Albert's backyard. The backyard where you poured gas on him and set him on fire."

Marianne started crying. She reached for a tissue and blew her nose and looked at Myers, deciding if she should say something. Instead, she laid her head on her arms.

"Here's the thing, Marianne. If you help us, by telling us everything – if you cooperate – well, I'll see if I can get the judge to reduce your sentence. Maybe, he'll let you out with just time served."

Marianne raised her head and gave Myers a questioning look. "Serious? You can do that?"

"I believe I can," Myers lied. "But you need to tell me everything."

"He wasn't supposed to hit him with a hammer," she said brokenly, through her sobs.

"What was he supposed to do?"

"When Albert and I went into the house, he was supposed to follow us."

"So, you planned on killing him inside the house? What did you plan to do to Albert?"

"I was supposed to get him undressed and then James - I mean Dr. Mont - was going to stab him and then we were going to set the house on fire."

"But he hit him with the hammer, so you changed plans?"

"We had to. When Albert saw James in the back seat he started to yell. James was afraid he'd wake up the neighbors, so he hit him a few times. I helped drag him to the backyard and we put him in the fire pit. James started him on fire."

"Where did Mont get the hammer? Did he bring it with him?"

"No. It must have been Albert's. It was lying on the floor in the car. It was – just handy, I guess you could say."

"Then, you and the doctor got in your car and drove away. Isn't that right, Marianne? After Mont bashed Albert's head in, poured gasoline on him, and set him on fire, you just went on your merry little way."

"It wasn't like that. You make it sound so cruel," she said.

"What was it like? It seems pretty damn cruel to me."

"We were avenging the death of James' son. Albert had to pay for his part in Peter's death. They all had to pay."

"What about Emma Lockhart? Did you kill her, too? Or, did Mont do that?"

"We didn't kill Emma. She killed herself."

"You called her and asked her to meet you in Forest Valley Park. You took a scalpel with you and you slit her wrists, didn't you?"

"I helped her. I put her out of her misery. She was never the same after the fire. I don't think any of us were."

"Emma didn't like blood, Marianne. She would have killed herself with pills, not by cutting her wrists."

"We meet and we talked for a while. I explained to her that she had to pay for what she had done. She made up that stupid game and then Albert cut Henry in the stomach and chest with that scalpel. None of that would have happened if she hadn't made up that game. And, because of her, Donna and Peter died.

They burned to death."

"It was an accident," Myers said. "No one planned for anyone to get hurt."

"I smelled Albert's flesh burning. It's a horrible smell. Peter and Donna smelled like that when they burned to death, you know. Emma deserved to die. So did Albert and Sarah."

"Whose idea was it to burn Albert's body?"

"It was James' idea. He thought of it after Emma died. He said that from now on we should burn them, just like they burned his Peter."

"Did you cut Emma's wrists, Marianne?"

"I helped her a little. We both held the knife and I helped her. She didn't mind. She said she wanted to die. I told her to close her eyes and pretend she was going to sleep."

"You just left her there while she bled to death. How could you have done that?"

"Don't you get it, Detective? It's called justice. Finally, we could get some closure. We were never going to hurt Wendy, of course. She didn't do anything wrong."

"So, Mont and you planned to kill everyone except Henry and Wendy. Is that right?"

"We would have, too, if that idiot brother of

James' had done his job. He got impatient."

"Were you in on the attempted murder of Brad?"

"What do you mean when you say in on?"

"Did you help them plan on how it should go down?"

"I was not part of that at all," Marianne said, emphatically. "That was all James and his brother, Robert. I had nothing to do with it."

"Were you aware of it?"

"Of course. James told me everything that was going on. But I didn't have anything to do with it."

"Robert paying someone to leave that card at Brad's house was clever. It really scared him."

Marianne smiled. "Did you really like it?"

"Absolutely," replied Myers.

"I wrote that poem. James thought it was so clever."

"Who helped Robert kill Sarah? Was it James?"

"Oh, no. No one helped him. It was just Robert. It was James' idea, though, that he use two different knives. You know, to confuse the cops."

"You're doing a really good job here, Marianne. You're really helping me."

"You're going to speak to the judge, right? Like you promised?"

"I certainly am going to let him know that you cooperated with us. In fact, I'm going to give you a pad of paper and a pen and ask you to write all this down. When the judge sees how much you helped us by putting exactly what happened in your own words, he'll be extremely pleased."

"Okay," she said, softly. Marianne shook her head a little. "I'm so tired. Is there any way I can get another cup of coffee?"

"In a minute. We're almost done here," replied Myers.

Thirty-four

"I can't believe you've lived in Kalispell all your life and you've never been to The Water's Edge Restaurant," Detective Myers said. "You're going to love it, especially this time of the year. They go all out with the Christmas decorations, and there are usually carolers wandering around downtown Somers, singing their hearts out. It's extremely festive."

"What are the restaurant's specialties?" she asked.

"Steak and ribs. I was thinking about having the ribs, but they are a little messy. I'll probably stick with the steak. A great big porterhouse sounds good right about now."

"I'm looking forward to it. The place sounds nice."

"I reserved a table by a window, overlooking the lake. It's really pretty with all the bright colored lights shining in the water."

She laughed a little and looked over at Myers. "I never, in a million years, would have taken you for a sentimental guy. It's nice to see this side of you."

Myers smiled and glanced over at her. "Being a cop is only part of who I am."

"Eyes on the road, Detective. It's snowing and we

don't need to end up in a snowbank."

"Sorry. It's just that you're so darn pretty, I can't take my eyes off of you."

"Am I just too good to be true? Are we really reciting song lyrics now?" she said, laughing.

Myers laughed and said, "Maybe you are. Too good to be true, that is. Guess I'll just have to wait and find out."

"Not to get too serious here, Myers, but what . . "

"Whoa. You can call me by my first name, you know."

"Morris," she said, and then repeated it. "I don't like that name. Morrie, maybe? No, I don't like that either. You know what? How about I call you Bill?"

Myers laughed again. "Just call me Myers. I'm okay with it."

"Okay," she said. "Bill, it is," making them both laugh.

"What were you going to ask me?" Myers inquired.

"It's not important," she said.

"No, go ahead and ask."

"I know the whole thing with the murders is over and all, but I'm trying to figure out why Marianne Pullman wasn't found not guilty by reason of insanity.

She had to be crazy to confess to murder and then plead guilty. The woman certainly has a few screws loose."

"Her defense attorney tried it. The judge determined that she was sane enough to be aware of what she was doing, so it didn't fly. She'll be spending a long time in prison for what she did. Maybe, she can get some help there."

"James Mont is going to die for what he did, isn't he?"

"Probably, but it will be years from now. There'll be loads of appeals, but eventually, the state will give him a lethal injection. Some convicts are in prison fifteen to twenty years before they use up all their appeals."

"I thought they hung 'em high here in Montana."

"They did," Myers said. "They changed that in 1955 to lethal injection. There hasn't been an execution since 2006. Do you mind if we change the subject?"

"I'm sorry I brought it up. It's just that Dr. Mont's trial is still so fresh in my mind."

"That's understandable. You were a big part of the trial. Let's just drop it for now and enjoy the evening," Myers said.

"You know I was really surprised when you called and asked me out. I never expected it."

"I thought long and hard about it before I picked up that phone. Plus, I had to wait for Mont's trial to end, and I wanted to give you a few weeks to get back to normal."

She glanced over at him once more and studied his face. She smiled to herself, thinking about how the evening was sure to end. There's nothing like a nice firm, experienced older man, she thought.

"A penny for your thoughts?" Myers asked her.

"Just thinking about that nice big piece of meat I'm going to enjoy tonight," she said.

"You do mean the steak, don't you?" Myers said laughing.

"Why, what else would I mean?" she said, teasingly.

He looked at her. "I have a feeling this is going to be one hell of a night."

"Will you please keep your eyes on the road?"

"Yes, ma'am."

"And, quit calling me ma'am."

About the Author

I was born in Idaho in 1939. My father's job demanded that we frequently move so, by the age of ten, I had lived in Idaho, Montana, Colorado, Michigan, and, finally Wisconsin. I lived in Wisconsin for the next eight years, until I graduated from school.

I am the proud mother of three wonderful sons and two fantastic grandsons.

I worked as an accountant for most of my life. Two years before I retired, I did a complete switch in careers and managed two Curves fitness facilities in Illinois. I retired in 2002 and moved to Branson, MO. In 2012, I moved to Indiana to be closer to my family and have lived in Highland for the past three and a half years.

I enjoy a good laugh and figure it's my sense of humor that has kept me going when times were tough. Reading has always been one of my passions and I still read a couple of books a week.

In 2003 I started designing websites for a few clubs and I maintain them in my spare time. I also designed my own site, so please feel free to visit.

For most of my life, I have written short stories and poems for amusement. I wrote *Blueberries and*

Bears and My Brother's Shoes, a book about growing up in the forties and fifties. After I self-published it and gave it to friends and family to read, they encouraged me to get serious about my writing.

Crossing Sydney was my first novel and it was published in July 2015. It has received outstanding reviews. A sequence to this book is being considered at this time.

Don't Smother Your Mother was my second book, and I had fun writing it. Although it's a mystery, I threw humor into it and made it an easy-to-read whodunit. *A Bad Week in Hollister* picks up where *Don't Smother Your Mothe*r leaves off, with another mystery for Sheriff "Cowboy" Berkson to solve.

Let's Play Autopsy takes place in Kalispell, Montana. At one time in my life, a long, long time ago, I lived there. Writing this book took me back to some of my childhood memories. The house I lived in is still standing, although it looks a little worn. But, then, so do I. I guess we could all use a new coat of paint.

I never thought that, at the age of 76, I would become an author. I certainly am enjoying my retirement knowing, that when I get up each morning, I have something to look forward to. You can find out more about me and my books at www.susanlpare.com.

Susan L. Pare'